The Cronus Cypher

The Cronus Cypher

Also by Hal Burton

Cave of Secrets

The Penny Red Enigma

Voices from the Mountain

Tubal Cain

Crescent Gold

Novelettes

The Mound

A Gandy Dancer's Tale

The Cronus Cypher

Hal Burton

FMH L.L.C.
Shelton, Washington

The Cronus Cypher

Although many of the names, places and events are historically true and used to add colorful background to the story, *The Cronus Cypher* is a work of fiction and the incidents and characters are products of the author's imagination. Any resemblance to persons living or dead is purely coincidental.

Printed and bound by Gorham Printing
Centralia, Washington

Produced and Distributed by FMH L.L.C.
Shelton, Washington

First Edition, First Printing – September 2010

Cover Design – by Kathy Campbell
Gorham Printing

Author photo by Jeanette Burton

Library of Congress Control Number: 2010909146

ISBN 978-0-9725707-1-8

Introduction

The Cronus Cypher is an imaginary tale; however, the significant incidents and personal experiences of the protagonist, Herschel Payne, are in great part taken from and based on Melvin Williamson's memoir, "A Journey of One … and More."

Mr. Williamson's memoir, published in 2009, chronicles his life from birth in Elma, Washington in 1935, to 2008.

I have selected the twenty years of Mel's service in the United States Navy to be the focal point of this story, but have used many of his boyhood recollections where they enhance the tale.

The real Herschel Payne was Mel's uncle and when selecting names for the fictional roles, it seemed fitting the leading character be named after someone with whom Mel had shared a special bond.

The Cronus Cypher

Espionage – *the practice of spying or using spies to obtain secret information about the plans and activities of a foreign government. Webster's Dictionary*

Photo # USN 1129208   USS Pueblo (AGER-2) off San Diego, California, 19 Oct 1967

USS *Pueblo*

Prologue

On January 23 of 1968 the USS *Pueblo*, a Navy intelligence vessel, was engaged in routine surveillance of the North Korean coast when it was intercepted by North Korean patrol boats. Although the United States claimed the *Pueblo* was in international waters, the North Koreans turned their guns on the ship and demanded its surrender. Though lightly armed, the Americans attempted to escape. The North Koreans opened fire, wounding the commander, Lloyd Bucher, and two others. With capture inevitable, the Americans stalled for time, destroying the classified information while taking further fire.

Finally, the *Pueblo* was boarded and taken to Wonson. There, the 83-man crew was bound, blindfolded, and transported to Pyongyang, where they were charged with spying.

On December 23, 1968, exactly eleven months after capture, U.S. and North Korean negotiators reached a settlement. The U.S. apologized for its actions after admitting the ship had been in North Korean territory. The surviving 82 crewmen were released and walked one-by-one across the bridge at Panmunjon to freedom in South Korea.

Much has been reported about what happened to the crew during their incarceration – the torture during hours of interrogation, severe beatings, food deprivation, and constant threats of death. "Confessions" to "criminally aggressive acts" were obtained from all the crew.

What was not known until recently, however, is that the *Pueblo's* mission and its planned course had been communicated in advance to the North Koreans by a spy within the sphere of the National Security Agency, an experienced communications technician and cryptologist.

The Cronus Cypher

Who They Are

Herschel Payne	Retired Chief Petty Officer - US Navy
Barbara Payne	Herschel's Wife
Spencer Winslow	Senior Agent - National Security Agency
Gerri Jennings	NSA Profiler
Woody Floyd	Retired Senior Chief Petty Officer
Russ Collins	Master Chief Petty Officer
George "Chief" Callgrove	Senior Chief Petty Officer
Michael "Mick" O'Brien	Master Chief Petty Officer
Jacob Harding	Director IA Section, NSA
Mark Payne	Herschel & Barbara's Son
Bruce Payne	Herschel & Barbara's Son
Melanie Payne	Herschel & Barbara's Daughter
Andy Hetzel	Navy Corpsman
Hae-won	South Korean Embassy Secretary
Ki-Woon	South Korean Legation Attaché
Jon ta Sun	North Korean Defector
Frank Stiles	NSA Agent – Washington, D.C.
Larry Burrows	NSA Agent – Seattle, Washington

Part One

"We live in deeds, not years:
        In thoughts, not breaths;
 In feelings, not in figures on a dial;
We should count time by heart-throbs.
        He most lives,
Who thinks most, feels noblest,
        Acts the best."

Bailey

Payne Residence – Montesano, Washington

One

The drive from our house on East Kamilche Avenue to Beacon Avenue Elementary School would take only a few minutes. Of course that usually depended on whether our eight-year-old Chevy Impala got us that far before sputtering to a stop or spontaneously jerking forward, and then stalling. "Big John" our twelve year old 1963 Chevrolet station wagon had not yet arrived from Scotland, so we were still driving the sedan we'd dubbed "Johnetta."

It had always been a tricky time driving the Impala, especially on our first trip, the journey north to the city that would become our first stateside home after my retirement.

Unbeknownst to me and the Astoria, Oregon dealer, who'd said, "I have no clue what that button on the end of the turn-signal does", the car had a retrofitted "speed control" unit. By the time we arrived in Montesano, I'd in some measure mastered the cruising feature, but now, it seemed to have developed a mind of its own, often popping into and out of operation whether activated or not.

The traffic light at Satsop Street turned red.

"Daddy, we're going to be late. I'm supposed to be in the choir room to warm up at three."

"Only four more blocks, you'll make it," I answered confidently, but praying I could find a parking spot this late.

Today was the fifth and sixth grade's choir concert at Beacon Elementary, the first for our fifth-grader Melanie, and she'd been talking about it nonstop for weeks. Our whole family loved the arts, especially music, and I was proud another Payne was following in my footsteps. Some of my memories concerning music weren't so pleasant, however, like the time Uncle Charles turned a stubborn ten year old over his knee for a good spanking when he wouldn't practice his piano lessons. I was Melanie's age, come to think of it.

Thinking of Melanie, I was about to mention we wouldn't have gotten such a late start if our daughter hadn't been rearranging her blond locks every five minutes, when Barb interrupted my train of thought.

"You should have left work earlier, Herschel, that Hoquiam and Aberdeen traffic is always bad, especially when it's been pouring like it has."

"I know, dear, but I had to turn in the money to Mike from the collection I made at the mobile home park in Westport."

Barbara didn't respond, but I could tell she was equally anxious as Melanie. After twenty-one years, you know how to interpret your spouse's body language.

"Dad, see that black car that's behind us?" Nineteen-year old Mark asked, tapping me on the shoulder.

I glanced in the rearview mirror as the light changed to green. "Yeah."

"It's been following us ever since we left home."

"You've been watching too much television, Mark," Barbara said, looking askance at Mark over her glasses.

"But Mark's right, Mom," his younger brother Bruce chimed in, pointing out the rear window, "that Plymouth's been on our tail for blocks."

"C'mon you two, that's enough. I agree with your mom, it's time for more 'Happy Days' and less 'Kojak' and 'Baretta'. Oh, here we are, and look, there's a spot to park."

Two

The '72 Plymouth Valiant stayed on Beacon Avenue when the Payne family turned left into the school's parking lot. National Security Agency profiler Gerri Jennings twisted around in the passenger's seat, watching the Impala as it disappeared from view behind the two-story brick building.

"Now what, Spence?"

Senior Agent Spencer Winslow hunched his shoulders and continued driving. They'd left the NSA office in Seattle that morning, planning to arrive in Montesano by noon, but they missed the turn to State Highway 8 and Grays Harbor, took US Highway 101 instead, and ended up north of the city of Shelton before realizing their error.

Winslow slowed and pulled into a curb three blocks past the school. "Guess we'll double back and watch the car, hopefully, they'll head back home." He slammed his fist on the padded dash. "Damn, one wrong turn. I should have checked the map better. At least we got to the house in time to see him leaving."

"Anyone would have missed that turn with the rain coming down like it was, and besides, I should have argued more about phoning him first, his profile seemed to indicate he'd be cooperative."

"No, Harding felt a face-to-face, unannounced meeting was best. If anyone's to blame it's me for not pushing him harder."

Jennings, who, as one of few female NSA agents, rarely showed any emotion or made personal contact, uncharacteristically reached across and softly patted Winslow's arm. "My fault, too. You don't think he spotted us, do you? I guess it wouldn't matter, but he might get spooked."

He took a deep breath and pulled away. "No, I stayed back, and who'd think anyone was following them in this Podunk town. There's something going on at that school, lots of cars. Let's find his Chevy and see what happens. Maybe you can go in and nose around."

"Hey, I'm the profiler, remember, not the field agent," she said, refastening her seatbelt. "I'll stand out like a sore thumb in this dark-blue suit."

He glanced to his right thinking how she'd stand out anywhere. It was hard to miss the strawberry-blond hair, especially when it topped a five-foot eight frame, and not even the conservatively cut blue-serge suit could hide that a curvaceous female form was beneath. Quickly, he looked away, and turned into the parking lot.

"Okay, there's his car, I'll let you out and then try to find a spot to park. Soon as what's going on is over, page me and I'll pick you up."

"Sure these new gadgets will work?" she answered, patting the pager in her jacket pocket.

"They'd better; Harding said the department's spent a bundle on 'm. Now, get going."

"Hope you find a spot to park the car," the hard 'a' in her pronunciation of car giving a hint to her New England origins.

Winslow found a parking spot four blocks away. *Finally*, he thought, rolling down the window and lighting a Marlboro. He'd been trying for weeks to break the habit, especially since Gerri was vehemently anti-smoking, but now, *screw it!*

Inhaling deeply and blowing an almost perfect smoke ring, he relaxed for the first time since they'd landed in Seattle. He looked at his watch – "probably be a while," he said out loud. Reaching behind to the back seat, he grabbed the thick envelope labeled "Operation Cronus". He'd read all five dossiers several times – amazed at the attention to detail. He removed the top dossier: thirty-one pages on retired Chief Petty Officer Payne's life before and during his naval career, and two photos. The first picture showed Herschel Payne in April 1968, shortly after he received his promotion to Chief Petty Officer. The picture was black and white, but it appeared Payne had blond hair and was fair-skinned, about five ten to eleven.

The second picture was more recent, taken of Payne and his wife, Barbara, at a Navy Day Ball, held in Stonehaven, Scotland, at the Stonehaven Inn in October of 1971. He hadn't changed much in three years, still had his handsome, boy-next-door looks. This picture confirmed his blond hair and fair skin. Payne very much resembled the movie actor Van Johnson in a film about a battleship during the Korean War, but Winslow couldn't remember the name of the movie. He did remember he was around ten years old when he saw it.

His wife, Barbara, appeared to be about Payne's age, maybe a few inches shorter. In the picture taken at the ball, her dark auburn hair was nicely styled for the gala in an "up-do."

Winslow lit another cigarette and began to read …

Herschel Payne was born in Elma, Washington in 1935. His parents, Ben and Myrtle Payne married in 1930 and Herschel's older brother Larry had been born three years later. The parents divorced when Payne was eight, just after the war started, and over the next several years the boys lived with several friends and relatives …

He closed the folder. *So I was wrong. Not the first time.*

"What … I'll be damned, they do work!" Winslow pushed the button to stop the vibration and started the car.

Three

My smile broadened as the choir began their last number, "The Lost Chord."

"Seated one day at the organ ..."

Almost twenty years earlier my grade school choir in Elma had performed the same classical piece. One of the most enjoyable classes I took in school was chorus. Unlike Melanie, however, who even now possesses a beautiful soprano voice, my vocal range had been much lower, even at eleven years, and today it was difficult for me to not hum along and help the four pubescent boys singing bass.

"Hersch," Barbara said quietly, putting a finger in front of her lips. "Ssh."

I nodded, but had continued to hum quietly. It helped take my mind off what had been bugging me since the concert began, a nagging feeling that my sons were right – the Plymouth had been following us. Too many years in the world of "spooks" had made me overly suspicious. It had, after all, only been a year and a half since I'd retired. A shiny new Plymouth following us in small town Montesano sure seemed strange – but, by the time we'd taken our seats, I began to believe my earlier pronouncement of, "too much television".

That was until the tall redhead in the dark-blue suit had walked into the auditorium. Most of the males in the audience had turned their heads as she took one of the two remaining seats in the front row, and those that didn't were either too young or very nearsighted.

Barb caught my glance as well as those of our two sons, and ignoring me, had leaned across and asked Bruce if he knew who the woman was. He shook his head. Mark too, shook his head, but gave me a wink.

I was about to comment when the choir, followed by the music teacher Miss Goble, had filed in and taken its place on the risers.

"… and I shall hear the grand Amen."

As we rose and clapped loudly with the rest of the proud parents and families, I glanced in the direction of the stranger and found her looking right at me. She quickly turned away. The man in front of me briefly moved in my line of vision and when I looked again, she was gone.

"Mark, why don't you get the car while we wait for Melanie." I tossed him the keys. "Meet you outside."

During the drive home I checked the rearview mirror several times – no dark Plymouth, but what stared back at me was equally ominous – my father: his steely blue eyes, thick eyebrows and the distinctive Roman nose of the Payne family. I glanced in the mirror again; no it could be the face of my brother Larry. But, *my God it's me.*

The distraction of, *I've become my father*, plus Melanie's excited recapping of the concert belied any thoughts of intrigue I might have conjured up. That quickly changed when I turned onto Kamilche and spotted the Plymouth parked in front of our house.

"That's the car," Mark exclaimed loudly.

"I see it."

Two people emerged from the car, a man and a woman – the same woman that had looked so out-of-place at the school.

"Herschel, what's going on?"

"I don't know. Take the kids inside." I closed the car door and walked across the lawn to greet the strangers.

Four

The man looked to be about my age, a bit taller perhaps, with wavy black hair and a neatly trimmed mustache like actor Clark Gable's. In fact, other than a pronounced scar over his eyebrow he was the spitting image of the character Gable played in *Run Silent, Run Deep*, one of my favorite war movies, right down to his leather Eisenhower jacket, which seemed out of character considering his white shirt and dark four-in-hand knotted tie. Up close, the woman was even more striking than when I'd first seen her at the school. She was slightly taller than the man and probably in her mid to late twenties.

"Can I help you?" For sure a lame question under the circumstances, but I couldn't think of anything else to say as they approached and stopped in front of the stone steps leading to the front porch.

"My name is Winslow, Chief Payne," he said, flipping open his wallet revealing an ID card I was familiar with, but hadn't seen in several years. "Agent Spencer Winslow and this is Agent Gerri Jennings, also with NSA."

"Retired Chief," I said, "what can I do for you, and by the way, why all the subterfuge?"

"We were going to call ahead, but decided not to, and then got here just as you were leaving …"

Winslow interrupted his partner. "Yes, we could have called, but …"

"C'mon, you can do better than that," I said, feeling somewhat bolder. "A simple phone call would have sufficed, besides, it's a Friday, and I might not have been here."

"We had information that you would be home, listen, I'm sorry, we need your help on something crucial to national security. Can we go inside and talk?"

I looked from one to the other. They were serious. "Sure, but I can't imagine how I can help …"

"Listen to what we have to say, and I think you'll understand," Winslow said, motioning toward the house, where I saw Barbara, Mark, Bruce and Melanie peeking out the living-room window.

"My family?"

"We should talk in private, Chief," Jennings said, noticing our observers too, and breaking into a smile for the first time. "We'll see how much they need to know later."

Barbara had told the children to go into the kitchen by the time we walked in, but stood firmly in the way just inside the door, hands on her hips. The look on her face reminded me of the day in Morocco I'd forgotten to tell her we were not to leave our home, and after she'd finished her cake decorating class at the embassy in Rabat, she'd been summarily escorted to the city limits. She looked at me, then the two agents.

"Hersch?"

"These agents are from NSA. Winslow and Jennings, and they need to talk to me for a while, nothing to worry about." I looked at Winslow for affirmation.

"Ma'am, we're sorry to bust in on you and your family." He motioned toward the living room. "If you don't mind?"

Barb again looked at one agent, then the other. "Fine, I'll be in the kitchen." She hesitated, "Coffee?"

"That would be great," Jennings said, following Winslow into the room, "let me know when it's ready and I'll come and get it."

I could tell that Barb was about to say something like, "This is my house and I'll bring it to you when it's good and ready", but she must have had second thoughts, for she smiled and walked away.

"Have a seat." I pointed to our new three seat leather couch on the wall opposite the bay window. "You've got the floor agent Winslow." I almost laughed at my little witticism.

"Spence will be fine, Chief … ah, Herschel."

He offered me his hand, but somehow calling him 'Spence' didn't seem quite right at this juncture.

Agent Jennings sat on the other end of the couch and I sat in my La-Z-Boy as Winslow turned to his partner, hand outstretched.

29

Five

"Let me see the file, Gerri."

For the first time I noticed Gerri Jennings was carrying a briefcase. "Here." She removed a manila folder and handed it to Winslow.

"I'll read this report to you first and then we'll fill you in on some of the details. Hold any questions, and Chief ... ah Herschel, and understand, it's top secret."

I sat quietly, in wonder, as he read.

"Two months' ago a North Korean intelligence agent, Jon ta Sun, defected to the United States. He revealed that for years North Korea had received classified information about our military and intelligence agency operations around the world, including: the Bay of Pigs incident, the Cuban Missile Crisis, our para-military operations in Laos, advance knowledge of the USS *Pueblo's* course, Operation Freedom Train in Vietnam, Operation Ivory Coast, the top secret OPLAN 34A, and the SAM Missile Intercept Mission in 1972. The information had come from a mole inside Naval Intelligence, code name 'Cronus.'

The Cronus Cypher

"Using the information given by Sun, my team and I began matching the dates of the covert transmissions to the naval personnel who would have had access to the information. The transmissions started in 1957. Each of the suspects were Naval Communications Technicians, specialists in cryptology, had worked at NSA, and been stationed at naval communications bases around the world during this time."

Winslow paused and looked at me. "You were on our first list."

"But I got out in '73."

"I know, and that's what we figured, especially when he told us about the message that's got everyone in a state of panic. It was received by the North Koreans just two days before Sun defected. You couldn't have known about it."

"I don't understand?"

An awkward moment of silence ensued. I stood up. "What in …"

"Let me go on … ah," he looked up and there was Barbara standing in the arched doorway with a tray in hand. "How long have …"

"Don't worry," Barb said, "I was a Navy wife for twenty years. Here's your coffee." She set the tray down on the coffee table next to me, did an almost perfect about-face and left the room.

We poured ourselves some coffee and Winslow continued. By now I had many questions, but reluctantly held back.

"After eliminating you from the list, the remaining four suspects are: Senior Chief Petty Officer Woody Floyd, Master

31

Chief Russell Collins, Master Chief Michael O'Brien and Senior Chief George Callgrove."

I almost dropped my coffee. "You've got to be kidding!"

"Hold on, Herschel, there's more." He hesitated. "Listen, let's take a break."

"Okay … ah … I need a cigarette, anyway."

"You too, huh, been trying to break the habit," Winslow said. He glanced around, then at me.

"No ashtrays. Since Barbara quit, it's the front porch or nothing. C'mon." Jennings stayed seated.

"Light?" I asked, as we sat on the stone porch bench. He nodded and I flicked the Ronson Delight I'd owned since I bought it on shore leave in Yokosuka ... *wow, almost ten years ago*, I thought … *I was with Woody – no, he can't be a spy* ...

I turned to Winslow. "Are you sure that Woo … "

"Let's just enjoy our smoke, I've got more to tell you, and then I'll answer your questions."

"**E**ach of these men had access to all of the data that was sent to the North Koreans, up to and including the latest. One possible exception is Chief Floyd, who recently retired, but he could have accessed the information last month and sent it later. This particular material is what has everyone on high alert." Winslow looked up from his notes. "The Koreans were sent President Ford's full itinerary for the upcoming conference in Helsinki. This classified information had been sent from Washington, D.C. to our embassies in London, Bonn, Paris and Helsinki."

I had to interrupt. "But his itinerary can be changed."

"Yes, and it has, but with just a week or so to go before the conference starts, if the mole is still active – well, who knows what they may be planning. The North Koreans would like nothing better than to keep the cold war going between the Communist bloc and the West."

"That should eliminate Woody Floyd from the list," I ventured, somewhat rhetorically.

"It should, but my bosses at NSA think possibly two of the men have been working together."

I shook my head. "Now this is really getting bizarre. So, even if this is all believable, and I'm not saying I buy it, where do I fit in?"

Jennings, who'd been quiet throughout Winslow's dialog, rose and stretched. "We believe you can help us discover the identity of the mole."

"Look," Winslow said, "it's late and we need to check in at the motel and get some dinner. Gerri's going to give you the file on each of the four men and a copy of the report I just read. Read them over tonight and we'll be back here at eight tomorrow. Chief Payne, Herschel, we need your help. We'll tell you our plan in the morning – hopefully, you'll agree."

"Do I have a choice?"

"Sure, but as a man who has proudly served his country for so many years, I think you'll choose to serve once again."

I nodded and walked with them to the door. "Where are you staying?"

"The Plum Tree Motel," Gerri answered. "Give us a call if you need to, otherwise, we'll pick you up around eight. And Herschel, reveal as little information to your wife as possible – okay?"

Six

I sniffed and inhaled. *Definitely a pie or cake in the oven.* At the Payne house we occasionally had dessert first and realizing how hungry I felt, was about to suggest that choice. After placing the files on the fireplace mantle, I walked into the kitchen.

"Smells great."

"Your <u>friends</u> are gone?" Barb said.

"Yup, gone until tomorrow morning. Where are the kids?"

"Don't change the subject. You look like the proverbial 'cat that swallowed the canary'."

"They told me not to discuss anything, I …they want me to help them, ah …discover who might be a spy, that's all I can say, for now."

"A spy!" said Bruce, coming into the kitchen. "Wow, Dad, are you going to do it?"

This was just the kind of drama our sixteen-year-old thrived on. "Maybe, that's enough information for now … "Call your brother and sister – dinner's on the table. And Bruce, let's not talk about this at dinner, okay?"

After dinner I retrieved the four files and went out on the front porch. It was a mild, balmy evening for mid-June, almost too warm, and as a consequence, most of the rhododendrons on the large bush by the porch were fading from lustrous dark purple to pale red, almost matching the hue of the sun's rays colored by smoke from a forest fire between us and Ocean Shores.

For me, a cigarette's always tasted the best after a meal, and even though I was trying to break the habit, I succumbed. Barbara had stopped some time ago and when she bugs me about smoking, I remind her of that time in 1958 when I was stationed at Fort Meade and we lived in Bowie, Maryland.

We had been snowed in for five days – no cigarettes, and Barbara pleaded with me to walk into Bowie to the only grocery store likely open on a Sunday. I hadn't needed boots in Japan, so in order to trudge through the two-foot snowdrifts, I wedged my feet into Barbara's ankle high fur-lined boots. The next obstacle for the nicotine-craved couple – we were short on cash. The only money we had were two rolls of pennies I'd been saving to start a coin collection.

I'll never forget that trek, and the shock of seeing a "closed" sign on the grocery store window. After a long, arduous walk through the snow for almost two miles, I'd been forced to backtrack to a small tavern I'd spotted a half-mile back. Fifteen minutes later, I approached the tavern. I was thankful to hear the sound of a band playing. Upon opening the door, a blast of hot air greeted me, along with at least two-dozen black faces. It was a "colored" tavern.

A very large black woman approached and asked what I wanted. When I told her cigarettes and that I only had two rolls of pennies, all she said was, "are they all there?" I nodded and she gave me the quarters for the machine. With two packs of Camels in hand I beat a hasty departure to a chorus of "what's that white kid in the funny boots doin in here?"

What a memory.

I knocked off the remaining ashes, field stripped my smoke, and picked up the files.

Each file was labeled with their names: Woody Floyd, George Callgrove, Russ Collins and Michael O'Brien. I still couldn't accept the fact that one of them was a spy for the North Korean's.

I thought back to when I had first met each man, and where we'd served together during my twenty-plus years in the Navy. Each file was labeled with "Operation Cronus" and the man's name. I had a vague recollection of what "Cronus" meant, and Winslow had confirmed – Cronus was a Greek God, the father of Poseidon and Zeus. Perhaps an odd code name for the spy to pick – maybe not, considering he was a navy man.

"I'll be damned," I said aloud, to no one in particular, and closed the first file, the one on Michael "Mick" O'Brien. I had forgotten that Mick and I first met at CT school at Imperial Beach, then were later stationed together at San Miguel in the

Philippines and Kami Seya in Japan. I racked my brain trying to remember the others in my communications class besides Mick.

Barbara opening the front porch door broke my train of thought.

"How much longer, Herschel? It's after eight and Melanie's ready for bed."

"I'll be in soon – say, do you remember who I used to talk about from Imperial Beach?"

She hesitated. "That was a long time ago, um … well, you always used to tell the story about buying that '42 Oldsmobile with some of your school buddies."

"Yeah, that's right. Wow, Jack Masterelli … ah, Andy Hetzel, Tony Mulinari, and," I reached for Russ's file, "Russ Collins! I'd forgotten completely about him being there."

"I'm surprised you forgot about your '42 Olds," she lay a hand on my shoulder.

"Thanks dear. Tell Melanie I'll be up to tuck her in."

Seven

The Bee Hive restaurant on Main Street had been recommended by the clerk at the motel and the waitress suggested the house specialty for the evening, 12-ounce prime rib. Agent Spencer Winslow was halfway through his well-done end-cut in no time. Gerri Jennings had opted for a lighter fare and ordered another specialty of the house, razor clams.

They'd said little about their mission since checking in at the Plum Tree, but now, she broke the silence. "Think he'll come on board?"

He looked up. "Payne? I think so, how about you?"

"Yes, but once you've told him everything, he may back out."

"You mean that we eventually want him to contact the men as we narrow down the list?"

"Yes."

"What about the possible connections to the Korean embassy in DC, and the strong probability that there's a link to a spy at the Seattle legation?"

"We'll see, not right away."

Winslow put down his knife and fork and gingerly wiped his mouth with the cloth napkin.

"Oops, you missed a spot." She touched her chin.

"It's all that great juice."

"Great tasting maybe, but not so great for your heart."

He nodded, and cut another thick piece of meat. "Gerri, you did the background research on him, he's going to want to see it through. He's always done what was expected of him, like the time you told us about when he lost his wallet in Yokohama and instead of lying, he admitted losing his Navy ID and liberty card, put himself on report, and took the consequences."

"I know, but this is different, he's a civilian now, with a wife and three kids."

"How about the wife?" Winslow asked before gobbling the balance of his prime rib. "Man, I could eat another one of these."

"She'll go along with the program, like any good navy wife."

"Don't be too sure. Dessert?"

"Nah," she checked her watch. "Got to watch my girlish figure, you know." Her smile brightened the freckles that bridged her nose. "Maybe we should head back?"

"Okay, but … think I'll have a slice of that blueberry pie." He waved at the waitress. "You sure you don't want some? Remember, the sign outside says 'Delicious Pies'."

Gerri shook her head, hesitated and said, "You were saying on the plane that your wife was a good cook …"

"Ex-wife." He moved back as the waitress brought the pie and cleared their dishes.

"How long?"

"Eight years, but it didn't seem that long." He smiled. "As the French say, 'c'est la viv'."

He took a bite of pie. "How about you, any long-term relationships?"

"No, with college, then the academy, I never had time for a 'long-term relationship.' Went with a guy at Cornell for a while, but since then, my romance has been with the NSA," she said, brushing her hand through her hair.

He looked up. Her azure-blue eyes were translucent, as if you could look deep into them, and that smile ... *damn, why does she have to be so beautiful?*

She caught his stare, held it, then turned away. *Watch it Gerri, you don't have time for this.* "We'd better get going, Spence, long day tomorrow."

Eight

Saturday in Montesano, Washington in June is much like any other day in Grays Harbor County in springtime – overcast, mid-fifties with a light drizzle, almost summer, but with a hint of winter still in the air. It was as if Mother Nature couldn't quite make up her mind. For me, however, this morning was decision time, pun notwithstanding.

I'd probably told Barb more than I should have, but if I was going to help Winslow and Jennings, and I still couldn't see how I might, she deserved to know the whole story; after all, she'd been with me through thick and thin – eight duty stations in twenty years.

I drank the last of my lukewarm coffee and set the cup next to me on the top porch step.

Before I'd retired for the night, I thoroughly perused each of the files and reread Winslow's report. Ironically, this morning's *Aberdeen Daily World* had a lengthy article about the upcoming conference in Helsinki, Finland. Thirty-five states, including the USA, Canada and most all the European states were attending. The meeting was called the Conference on Security and Cooperation in Europe. It said that both President Ford and Secretary of State Kissinger would attend.

I looked at my watch. *Seven-fifty, they'll be here soon.* I had many, many questions, but I'd ninety percent decided to do what I could to help. One major question that sticks in my craw is that if one of the four is a spy, "the mole," how he can be transmitting secret information from different locations, at different times to North Korea? There has to be some intermediary.

I heard the car before I saw it. "Right on time," I said aloud as the Plymouth pulled up. I stuck my head in the door. "Barbara, they're here."

"Good morning." I walked down the steps. *Well, here goes.*

Winslow extended his hand and Jennings smiled.

"C'mon in."

"Herschel, we'd like to go to our motel and continue there, that's if you're with us on this?" Winslow said.

I looked from one to the other. "I am. I've got several questions, but, okay. I'll tell Barb and be right back."

The rooms at the Plum Tree Motel on Pioneer Avenue were decorated country style – knotty pine walls, metal sculptures of geese on the walls, a painting over each queen-sized bed depicting cowboys herding cattle and square lamp shades adorned with duck and cattail silhouettes. If it hadn't been for the busy carwash across the street you'd have thought you were staying at a quaint country inn. The only thing missing was a Charles Russell painting of an Indian on horseback.

Winslow sat in one of the two chairs, Jennings was perched on the edge of the bed.

"Before you ask any questions, let me tell you how we'd like to proceed – hopefully, it will make sense then and maybe give you some of the answers," Winslow said.

For the next several minutes Winslow revealed their plans.

We'd take each of the men under suspicion and I would try to remember everything I could about them, recall our times together, any missions we took, any unusual happenings, in essence, flash back to those earlier times in as much detail as I could. Occasionally they'd ask questions.

"Now, here's the catch," he said. "When we're all done, we want you to personally contact each man and … well, we'll explain that later."

"I really don't see how my reminiscing can help narrow down the list."

Jennings spoke for the first time since we'd gotten to the motel. "We'll be the judge of that, Herschel. With all your remembrances and our questions, I think you'll be amazed at what we can piece together."

"She's right, so, shall we get started?" Winslow said. "How 'bout we begin with Woody Floyd?"

Nine

"**I** was nearing the end of my tour of duty in Hawaii when I learned that CINCPACFLT was looking for a Communications Technician volunteer to accompany the aircraft carrier U.S.S. *Yorktown* to Japan for a reassignment of her homeport. I submitted my name – if accepted, it would be my first seagoing deployment. A few …"

"Excuse me Herschel, before you go on, what's CINCPACFLT?" Jennings asked.

"Commander-in-Chief of the Pacific Fleet, sorry, I'll try not to use too many Navy acronyms."

"A few days later I learned my application had been accepted and another sailor from Hawaii, First Class Petty Officer Woody Floyd, would be going, too. I'd known Woody since Radioman School at Imperial Beach in '54, we'd been together in the Philippines and he'd been in Hawaii several months, so I was a little more at ease about boarding an aircraft carrier with a crew of four-thousand. Good ole Woody, so he's out now, too. Jeez, that school seems like ages ago.

We had begun the Radioman School with thirty and twenty-four graduated. Let's see, Woody and I, Beth Mason, Jim Devers, Russ Collins, Andy Hetzel, and … that's all I can remember. I know I really sweated it out. We had to take at least eighteen words a minute of Morse code. If you didn't master at least the eighteen, you didn't graduate and move on to CT school … 'Communications Technician'. Every night I went to sleep dreaming dit, dah, dit, dah, dit. Drove me crazy."

"Did those people you remember from your class all pass and go on to CT school?" Winslow asked.

"Yeah, ah… yes, those ones did."

I continued my narrative.

"Three months later, I graduated from CT school, ah … that was in January 1955. Our class was designated 'O' branch, for Operations, which was my specialty within that branch of the Navy and we all were given a Secret clearance – all of us would be part of the Naval Security Group. Those who didn't graduate were immediately assigned to a ship, and with Barb pregnant with our first child, a lot was at stake."

"Did all the Radiomen pass the CT school?"

"No, only fifteen did."

Winslow continued. "Do you remember them?"

"I can't remember about Jim or Beth, but Woody and Russ did. Andy Hetzel didn't, but he became a medical corpsman.

"Okay, let's go back to Woody Floyd and your assignment on the *Yorktown*, let's see, that would have been in '66 about the time of Operation Diego Garcia." Winslow said.

"Yeah, I remember we were knee deep in messages during the trip, had us 'crypies' working overtime on setting up the link for the White Cloud satellite program."

Jennings's cleared her throat, as if to say, 'moving on'. "Woody's a black man isn't he, a Negro? I guess today's preferred name is African-American?"

"Yes he is ..." I looked her straight in her beautiful blue eyes. "And a great sailor and friend, too."

"I'm not implying he wasn't, ... ah ... isn't a great fellow, I ..."

"Why don't you go on, Herschel?" Winslow interjected, looking annoyed.

"All right. It took seven days to get to Japan. We docked in Yokosuka and that night Woody hooked up with a few African-American sailor friends he'd met on the *Yorktown* and I went out on the town with some swabbies I'd met."

"So you didn't see him again until you flew back to Hawaii?"

"Actually I did. On the way back to our barracks I spotted him standing alone on a street corner."

"Where – what part of town?" Winslow asked, showing excitement for the first time.

"I don't remember for sure, but he was glad to see me, I remember he'd had one too many beers and didn't know how to get back. He said his friends had wandered off."

"Okay, when did you see him again?"

"We flew back to Hawaii the next day, and, let's see, I left for the States and Cheltenham, Maryland a couple weeks later, ah ... don't think I saw him again after that."

Winslow stood and stretched. "Time for a smoke break. Gerri, why don't you see if you can round up some coffee? Then I'd like to go over some of the personal info on Floyd – see if you can add anything."

"Is what we're doing helping?" I asked, following Winslow out the door.

"Yes, every little bit helps."

Fifteen minutes later we were back in the room and Jennings had three cups of coffee ready for us.

She looked up at Spence. "I don't mind doing this once in a while guys, but next time it's someone else's turn — no more good girl Friday."

"You're right, sorry, I'll make the coffee run next time," Winslow said, turning to me. "Here, this is Gerri's profile of Floyd. Look it over while we have our coffee. I know you looked at it yesterday, but a review never hurts."

The profile was quite detailed and covered things I didn't know about Woody. His dad was African-American, his mom, Japanese. His dad had been in the Army during World War II and had been stationed in Japan after the war. His last station was at Fort Meade. He was single and failed the Master Chief test three times. As far as NSA knew, no one had been in contact with Woody since he had been forced to retire.

"Can you add anything?" Gerri Jennings asked me.

"No, maybe I'll think of something later."

"Okay, how about your time with him in the Philippines?" Winslow said.

I hesitated, trying to think back to 1961, and smiled.

Winslow noticed. "What's so funny?"

"I hadn't seen Woody in almost seven years and then we spotted each other at a VD lecture." I tried not looking at Jennings.

She cleared her throat. "It's okay, Herschel, I'm a big girl."

"Anyway," I said, hoping I wasn't red-faced. "We endured the lecture, while the officer rambled on about how Subic Bay had the second highest incidence of venereal disease in the Pacific Theater, and then went out for a beer to get reacquainted."

"After that?" Winslow offered, showing no sensitivity to my embarrassment or seeing the humor of the moment.

"We became good friends and he and Barbara hit it off – we had him over to our place in San Miguel several times."

"What about at work? Do you remember anything out of the ordinary?"

"No … ah, he and I worked different shifts in the security group most of the time."

"So in summary, Floyd never was with you in Japan, Guam, or Scotland?"

"No, he may have served there at other times – you've got the records …"

"Okay, Herschel," she looked questionably at Winslow.

"All right, let's move on to Russ Collins. We'll come back to Floyd if we need to."

Ten

The telephone rang as I opened the file. Jennings and I sat quietly as Winslow held the receiver to his ear, occasionally saying "yes" or "I understand."

He replaced the receiver and turned to us. His face showed concern, a scar over his right eyebrow more prominent as he frowned. "That was Harding. Things are heating up, and we don't have as much time as we thought. NSA just decoded a message from Pyongyang to their embassy in Geneva. It said, "Helsinki operation in place, proceed as planned.""

"But doesn't that absolutely eliminate Woody as a suspect?" I quickly said.

"Maybe, but remember, we don't know where he is, and it's still possible there are two of them working together," Winslow said. "All right, we've still got some leeway – let's move on to Collins."

"Maybe this time we should let Herschel review my profile on Collins first."

Winslow looked at me. "Herschel?"

"Fine, I read it last night, but … yeah, that's a good idea."

The Cronus Cypher

Similar to the one about Woody, Jennings's report on Russ was thorough. He was my age and like me, married, but with just one child, a girl eight years old. He was similar in height and had blond hair. Russ was heavy into physical conditioning and frequented the gyms both on and off the bases. He had a juvenile record, which unfortunately for him led to the Naval Academy turning down his application in spite of his high IQ and lettering in two sports. Russ was from New York State. I'd served with him in Guam and at Fort Meade, as well as being with him in Boot Camp and at CT school.

I set the file down.

"Anything you can add about him personally?" Jennings asked.

"Russ is a bit of a hothead, and ... well no, I ... why don't I just go ahead and tell you what I remember from our days in Guam and at Fort Meade?"

"Okay." Winslow looked at his watch. "Almost one o'clock. Go ahead, then we'll break for lunch."

"Oh, I just remembered something, Russ and I used to talk about for hours during Boot Camp."

I caught Jennings's quick look at Winslow. He looked at me. "All right, who knows."

"We'd talk about our love for dogs, especially collies." I saw their blank stares. "No, listen, we were both loners as kids, no real close friends. He grew up on Lake Skaneateles in rural New York and I was by myself a lot – our best friends were our collie dogs. Mine was named Ring, for the white ring around his neck, his was named Argos – can't remember why, anyway ..."

"Herschel, we appreciate the boyhood tale, but I can't see any connection – let's move on to more recent times, okay?"

I shrugged my shoulders, a bit irritated at Winslow interrupting me. I hadn't thought of Ring for years, but realized I had wandered off the subject. "Okay."

"Russ and I were on the same flight to Guam and both had orders for the Naval Communications Station, which is near Agana. It was the first duty station for both of us, so we were pretty excited. I spent a lot of my spare time looking for a place to rent so I could bring Barbara over."

"She was pregnant, right?" Jennings asked.

"Yes, Mark was born three months later."

"How about Collins? He was single?"

"Yup."

"Did he go out a lot, spend time with the local ladies?"

"Not much, ah … he mostly spent time with the other swabbies, and …"

"He had other close male friends like you?"

"A couple, Andy Hetzel and, let's see, Jim Devers; actually we didn't see each other much after what occurred one evening when I missed the navy bus back to the base."

"What happened?" Winslow asked, sounding interested for the first time in a while.

"Well, as I said, I'd missed the last bus. It was getting dark and I'd been sticking my thumb out with no results when a pickup truck slowed, then stopped several yards ahead. I was really surprised when I reached the passenger door – there was Russ. He poked his head out and said to get in."

The Cronus Cypher

Winslow's slow tapping on the desk sidetracked me, and signaled he was getting impatient. "Didn't have to roll the window down, huh?" he said sarcastically.

"Nobody kept their windows rolled up in Guam unless it rained – too hot."

Winslow smirked. "Herschel, this still sounds like another da …"

"Just wait – I'm almost finished." The tapping stopped. "The guy driving the truck was in his early twenties, quite handsome, almost feminine looking …"

"You mean he looked like a homosexual, a queer?" Winslow said, almost snapping to attention.

"Yes, today, we'd say he looked gay, but sadly, back then using terms like queer and fag were much in vogue."

"You think Collins was gay?" Jennings asked.

"Well, I wondered, especially when he seemed to avoid me after that. But, when I was with him at Fort Meade, he was married, and so I figured I was wrong."

"We knew he was at Fort Meade when you got there in '68," Winslow offered.

"Yeah, we were both there and both were sent to Teletype Maintenance School in Norfolk."

Winslow and Jennings exchanged looks. Jennings spoke first. "So, he was there for sure when the *Pueblo* incident happened?"

"Yes – that was in your file," I answered, looking at her.

"Yes, as far as Fort Meade goes, but the records don't show he finished the school in Norfolk."

"As a matter of fact, I remember now, he didn't," I said. "Only about half did."

"Before you went to Norfolk, were you privy to the mission of the *Pueblo*?"

"Yes, all of the guys in crypto were."

"And that included Collins? Winslow asked.

"Yes."

Winslow stood. "Okay, let's break for lunch. We'll pick up on Chief Callgrove after that."

"What about tonight and tomorrow? It's Sunday and we usually go to eleven o'clock service at The United Methodist Church."

I realized the moment I'd spoken, it was a stupid question. "I'll call Barb and tell her not to expect me for dinner."

Eleven

As Winslow and I smoked our second cigarette, a light rain began to fall, not untypical for Grays Harbor in mid-June.

"How'd you get that scar?" I asked, not able to hold off my curiosity any longer.

"I could tell you it was during some secret mission, but that would be fibbing, big time. I got it when I was ten years old – walked into a backyard swing."

The rain increased in intensity and we moved close to the wall, under the roof overhang. As if on cue, the motel room door opened.

"All right you two, time to go to work. You both should kick the habit, anyway."

"You're a pest sometimes, you know Gerri," Winslow responded, but chuckled and stuck his smoke in the nearby sand-filled butt can. "Herschel, time to get at it."

When we entered, Jennings was seated on the desk chair holding a manila folder. "I'll read Callgrove's profile out loud and then you can add anything you can think of Herschel."

"Listen, just about everyone calls me Hersch, so let's go with that."

"Sounds good," Jennings said, how about same for us – Gerri and Spence?"

I nodded and she began.

"George Callgrove enlisted in 1956 in Rapid City, South Dakota. At his last physical he weighed in at 200 pounds, not good shape for his height of five foot six. His parents were both alcoholics and still live on the Pine Ridge reservation near the town of Wounded Knee. During the Wounded Knee uprising and occupation of the town in '73, Callgrove took leave and joined the civil rights protest. He was not arrested but was placed on report. This doesn't say why, but I checked into it, and he was reprimanded for wearing his uniform. Apparently he was spotted in one of the TV broadcasts. Probably cost him his promotion to Master Chief.

He married a Muslim woman he met in Morocco, but they've been divorced for two years. His one child, a boy lives with his ex in Rabat. He's due to retire this year. Callgrove's nickname is 'Chief', in deference to his Indian heritage rather than naval rank. Other than his dark skin, black hair and high cheek bones he doesn't look like your stereotypical Indian, but even as a Second Class Petty Officer, his friends called him 'Chief'."

"Hersch?"

I figured it was my turn and I didn't know where to start except at the beginning, as it's hard to describe Chief in just a few words, he was – is – a real character.

"As you've said, Chief was a bit shorter than most of us and even in 1957, must have weighed a hundred and eighty or so. I met him in the Gee Dunk …"

"Hersch, that's about the fifth time you've used that expression. What the 'H' is a 'Gee Dunk'?" Winslow asked.

"Oh – guess you weren't in the navy, so you wouldn't know. Sorry. It's the place where we bought snacks like ice cream, potato chips, candy, and soda pop. Guess you'd call it a commissary, or a store with vending machines."

"But geedunk, where did that name come from?"

"Never really knew while I was in – just what we all called it. I did ask a buddy one time and he said it's because that's the sound made by a vending machine when it dispenses pop in a cup, 'gee dunk!'"

"Weird – okay, let's move on." Winslow snickered. "Gee Dunk, I'll be damned."

"So as I was saying, Chief and I met in a gee dunk after our watch. We were assigned to the same watch and became great friends and on that particular day we took the bus to Yokohama and went bar hopping. Chief loved his beer, especially the Japanese beer, Kirin – it came in a 24-ounce bottle, and he could down three or four before I finished my first. While he was on his fifth, a fellow sat down next to him, and I'm not sure how, but Chief learned the guy was a Marine. I'm not sure who said what to whom, but suddenly Chief threw a haymaker at the gyrine – cold-cocked him so hard he was out for the count.

As it turned out this guy's buddies, who I assume were also Marines, crowded around Chief and he was ready to take on the whole lot. At some point I said something like 'Chief, we've got to go or we'll miss the last bus.' They must have thought he was a real Chief Petty Officer, or else decided not to take on the drunken, wild-eyed, muscular guy, because they backed off and I grabbed Chief and we got out."

"So Callgrove was hard to handle when he got drunk – wild, as you say?" Jennings asked.

"Yeah, but most of the time he'd sober up fast. One time, however, it cost him a lot. He got placed on report, received a Captain's Mast, like a court for enlisted men's minor offenses, and was restricted to base for a month."

Winslow nodded. "I've heard of that – had a friend who got two months for something or other. What'd Callgrove do?"

"Got mad one night when he couldn't open a side-by-side set of glass doors to get into the barracks, so he slammed his fist right through 'm. Several weeks later he was assigned to a different watch and I didn't see much of him after that. Messed up his arm badly – had to go to sick bay and get the lacerations stitched up."

"That was '57 or '58 … ah, so you didn't serve with him again until '69 when you went to Morocco?" Jennings offered.

"No."

"Did you notice in his file that he was at Fort Meade in '59?"

"Yes."

"Did he ever talk with you about Bernon Mitchell or William Martin when you were with him in Morocco?"

"Ah … who … oh, I remember. Those were the NSA guys that defected. No, but I do remember Mick O'Brien mentioning he knew Martin, called him 'Ham'."

"That was when?"

"At San Miguel in the Philippines, in '61."

"You didn't know either of them, then?" Winslow asked.

"No, they were civilians, math nerds, gone by the time I arrived at NSA."

"All right", Winslow said, "anything out of the ordinary happen in Morocco, concerning Callgrove?"

"Let's see, he was married when I got there, and, oh yeah, he and I ended up volunteering for a short stint on the *Galveston*. We flew from Rabat to Athens – met the ship there."

Jennings spoke. "So that was, what, in early '69, after the *Pueblo* crew was freed?"

"Yes, we were scheduled to cruise the Mediterranean from June to September."

"How close did you get to Libya?"

"We were in the Gulf of Sidra for several days in August."

"Ever hear of Operation Tripoli?"

I shook my head no.

"But you do remember when Gaddafi overthrew the monarchy – if you don't, it was on September 1st. We and the Brits were supporting the monarchy and somehow Gaddafi found out about our deployment, our troop strength and well, when his troops attacked the palace, we were outnumbered and eventually pulled out. According to the defector, Jon ta Sun, the North Koreans had gotten a detailed report on our troop strength and passed it on to Gaddafi."

"And you think the info was sent from the *Galveston*?"

"We don't know for sure," Winslow answered, "but it could have been."

Jennings turned to me. "I know it was a long time ago, and I'm constantly amazed by how much you do recollect, but do you remember any top secret communications regarding Libya or reference to Operation Tripoli?"

"Actually no, but I do seem to recall Chief was in sick bay for several days around that time. He'd been so shaky, that he kept tearing the tape trying to feed it into the transmission distributor on the 28-KSR. I doubt he would have had any info – as a matter of fact I remember Andy Hetzel, and another swabbie, ah … Terry Weston, and I playing poker with Chief – he was better, but still restricted to bed."

"Hetzel … I thought he'd washed out of CT school?"

"Yeah, he did. He and Weston were medical corpsmen, doing TDA on the *Galveston* just like Chief and I."

"You were still using the 28-KSR in '69 – wow, I thought most of the manual crypto machines had been upgraded to voice encryption by then."

"No, we used the KSR well into 1970."

Winslow stood, loosened his tie for the first time and pulled his pack of Marlboro cigarettes from his shirt pocket. "Let's take a break, and then we can get into O'Brien's file." He looked at me. "Smoke?"

The Cronus Cypher

Model 28-KSR Key Board Send-Receive

Twelve

It had stopped raining and the sun peeking under the tail of the elephant on the Pink Elephant Carwash sign cast a weird shadow pattern on the motel parking lot with each rotation. Agent Jennings had returned from a second trip to Gene's Stop-And-Go, this time for burgers, fries and shakes. I took a final drag on my smoke and thought to myself that this spy business is sure not helping a recently begun effort to stop my expanding mid-section, let alone my attempt to stop smoking.

We'd been into Mick's profile only a few minutes when the phone rang. It was their boss, the enigmatic Harding – who despite it being Saturday and well after quitting hours in the east was bringing his senior agent up-to-date. For me, it certainly brought home to bear that what we'd been doing was not an exercise in minutia.

I hadn't been able to tell from Winslow's expression whether he was hearing good or bad news, for as before, he was strictly a listener except for the occasional "yes", "no", or "I understand."

Before the last "I understand" he'd said, "Tomorrow at nine" and dropped the phone in its cradle before turning to face us, still not telegraphing any emotion in his expression.

"We need to get to Washington tomorrow."

I figured he meant DC. "You're leaving?"

"We all are – you included."

"What – you're not serious? I just can't drop everything and fly off to DC," I said, reacting like the civilian I now was, realizing I had a choice.

Jennings saved me from saying something I'd probably be sorry for. "What's happened?"

"They've been monitoring all communications to the South Korean embassy...."

"South Korea, I thought ..."

Winslow held up his hand, palm towards me. "I'll explain in a minute. Anyway, the newest decoded one says, 'Agents in place – Helsinki – waiting new itinerary for subject'."

Jennings recognized my frustration and ignoring Winslow's put-off, explained. "Hersch, what we haven't told you is we are almost one-hundred percent sure our mole has a contact at the South Korean Embassy, and therefore quite obviously someone at the embassy is also an agent for the North."

"So you've been intercepting all the traffic into and out of our allies' embassy?"

"Yup – a bit touchy, but necessary," Winslow offered, giving Jennings a cold look.

I shook my head. "Hopefully, they'll understand when we tell them."

"They'll have to, especially when we nab the mole in their midst. Diplomatic immunity won't matter. Listen, we need to move on. Here's what Harding wants."

I listened intently, but anxiously as Winslow detailed the plan.

Unrevealed until now, I learned that orders had already been sent to Mick O'Brien, Russ Collins and Chief Callgrove to report to Fort Meade on Monday. The telex stated that they were temporarily assigned to a special task force of senior communications technicians who would be handling message exchanges during the conference in Helsinki.

Russ Collins was currently in Hawaii, Chicf was instructing at CT school at Imperial Beach and Mick was already in DC at Fort Meade.

Part of the hastily-conceived plan had been to ask Woody to DC on some other pretense, but no one knew where he was. My role in the plan is to meet separately with each man and ... I couldn't hold back any longer.

"Okay, so we fly to DC and from what you hinted at before, I'll talk to each of them and ... what ... won't they be pissed when they find it's all a ruse?"

Winslow didn't look as mad as I thought he'd be for my interruption. In fact, he smiled. "But that's the thing, Hersch, it is and it isn't. We really do need some experienced help coding and decoding all the transmissions from Helsinki. Let me go on."

The plan was I would meet with each man; revealing to him I was working with NSA to help uncover the identity of a mole.

I slowly shook my head. "So you think that whoever the mole is will panic and in some fashion give himself away?"

"Yes."

"But why me?" I knew I was hooked at this point. "Guess you've got me convinced."

"As I've already said," frustration showing in his face, "you're going to tell each man, all navy friends of yours, what you've been doing with us, going back over all your associations with them, and tell them with their help we can uncover the mole's identity – that's the reason you're in DC."

"Won't Russ, Chief and Mick each put two and two together and realize they're under suspicion, I mean, give me a break, they'll surely see the connection to me – why I've been called in, I'm the one link."

"If they do, so much the better. Harding thinks our work here with you today will narrow down the list, so maybe we'll be closer when we get to DC."

I looked at each of them. "Has it – I mean have you narrowed down the list?"

"Not yet," Jennings said, "and what's really bugging me is that Woody could be our mole and working with one of the other three. That could shoot the whole plan down."

"All right," Winslow said, looking at his watch, "we've got a lot to do in the next twenty-four hours. Herschel we'll do whatever it takes to free you up for several days."

I laughed. "Oh, you're going to tell Barb. Good luck with that. You can explain it to my boss at the bank, too."

"You'll have to enlighten your wife, but if you need some help with your boss, I'm sure we can help there."

"Tomorrow is Sunday, you know?" I offered, sounding I admit, a wee bit sarcastic.

"Why don't we use what time we've got left today to finish up on Mick O'Brien? Who knows, you may remember something about him that will make our job a whole lot easier."

Thirteen

"**A**s I said before, Gerri, I can't add much to your profile of Michael O'Brien. As you accurately describe, Mick is a Boston-born and bred Irish Catholic with the red hair and temperament to match. I do recall his dad died when he was young. He, his brother and sister were raised by their mom. Oh yeah, he hated everything English – I think his dad had been a big IRA supporter, belonged to a couple Boston clubs with IRA connections to the mother country."

"That's it?" Gerri asked.

"Yes … no, there was something else … that's right, Mick loved to sing, probably still does. He and I both sang in the San Miguel Church Choir. Some of our buddies said he sounded like Bing Crosby, kinda looked like him too, except for the red hair."

I stood up and stretched. "That's it."

"Fine. Now let's get into your navy life with him," Winslow said, motioning to the chair.

I ignored Winslow, walked into the bathroom and filled a glass with water from the tap. Only after taking a good swallow did I return to the chair.

"Mick was in CT school when I started Radio school in '54. The next time I saw him was at San Miguel."

Jennings reached for her notes. "Hold on, weren't you with him in Japan?"

"No, he was there, but not at the same time. We were together for a while at Fort Meade also, but I remember him most from the Philippines, at San Miguel. Barbara wasn't there for about six months so I spent a lot of my free time with Mick and some of the other CT guys."

"Okay, go on," she said. Jennings glanced at Winslow who seemed to be preoccupied.

She cleared her throat.

"I'm listening," he said. "Just can't get all these different places fixed in my mind – the timelines all intertwine. It's confusing to say the least. Yes, go on Hersch."

"We went to the local beaches, swam, played volleyball and worked on our tans – once in awhile hitting the bars at a little village called Olongapo."

I paused. "You know I just remembered something that may help us."

I had Winslow's attention now.

"During one of our volleyball games I cut my foot really bad. Some native girls had been watching our game and seeing the blood gushing from my foot, rushed over, told me to wrap the gash with a towel, keep pressure on the wound and they'd be right back. They returned two minutes later, both chewing a large wad of green leaves. They pulled off the towel and put the wads on the wound. Amazingly, the pain subsided. They told me to keep the poultice on and it would stem any infection until I got to the base dispensary. We thanked them and Mick hailed a Jeepney to get us back to the base at San Miguel."

Jennings said, "Okay, I'm going to guess a 'Jeepney' was a local name for a Jeep."

I smiled. "Yes, after the war we abandoned many of our Jeeps and the natives fixed them up and used them for taxis."

"What's the great revelation, ah … what's the important thing here …?"

"I'm just about there, Spence," I said, using the more familiar handle.

"When we got to the dispensary the doctor said it was a pretty bad cut and would require many stitches. He called for a corpsman to assist him. Guess who showed up, Andy Hetzel.

I saw a lot of Andy after that – in fact about once a week for nine weeks. He helped me get used to my crutches which I had to use for three weeks, and then it was another six weeks before I could walk without limping."

"Hersch!" Winslow was getting anxious.

"Okay, okay. Andy and Woody became close friends over the years – served at several of the same duty stations, once at San Miguel. If anybody knows where he is, I bet Andy does! We got a Christmas card from Andy and his wife, and Barb has their phone number. I'll call tonight."

"Great. We probably should stop soon anyway, but I do want to cover one more area and that's what you remember about the Cuban Blockade. Were you and Mick working at the

Naval Security Group office together and were there top-secret communications about Cuba?"

"Man, that's a while ago – October 1962. I was, let's see, twenty-seven with two kids. I remember it was a very tense time for everyone, especially those of us with families. As far as messages, a lot of the secret stuff was when the U-2 first spotted the missiles."

"Had you and Mick known about the U-2 spy planes flying over Cuba?" Winslow asked.

"Yeah, just about everyone did in our security group. I'd known since 1958 about the existence of the plane and it really wasn't much of a secret, especially when the Russians shot down Powers in 1960. Both Mick and I decoded messages about the Cuban fly-overs.

When Kennedy made the announcement, we all figured it would be World War III. Barb and the other wives and dependants attended briefings on what to do if it started. We in communications were told to be ready to be taken off the island in subs."

"In subs! Hard to believe." Gerri reached out and touched my arm. "It must have been pretty scary, especially for the families. Thank God the Russians backed off." She turned to Winslow. "We'd better wrap it up. If Hersch thinks of anything else, we can continue our review on the plane tomorrow. Right now, we should get him home so he can pack and have time to contact Andy Hetzel and his wife about Woody Floyd."

"You're right. Hersch, we should get you back, and if you have it, give me your boss' phone number at the bank."

"I'll get it for you when I get back to the house."

Fourteen

The sun was setting behind our neighbor's garage as I slowly climbed the stone steps to our front porch.

I'd mentally rehearsed what I was going to say to Barbara during the time it took for Winslow and Jennings to drive me home from their motel, but with each upward step my resolve was fading. Barb had said she'd start dinner later than usual, and I was hit by the unmistakable aroma of a cooking ham and bread as I opened the front door.

"I'm home honey." No answer.

"Angel?" I called, using the endearing name I often called her.

"She's upstairs, Dad," Mark said as he bounced up from the sofa. "Melanie and Bruce went to Swanson's for some ice cream. They should be back soon."

"Smells like dinner's about ready. I'll see what your mom's up to."

Our second story has three bedrooms: Melanie's, ours, and one shared by the boys. When I reached the top of the stairs I was greeted by the sight of my Samsonite American Tourister luggage blocking any further progress to our room.

I pushed the suitcase aside and opened the door. "How'd you know?"

She was sorting clothes on the bed. "It wasn't hard to figure. How long?"

"A week at most … ah …"

"A week, you're sure?"

"Maybe a few days more. I'll know more after we've been there a few days."

"By 'there', I assume you mean Washington?"

"Yes, Fort Meade most likely. Listen there's something I need to do first and then I'll explain as much as I can."

"Dinner's ready." She gave me a look through her cat-eye glasses that would have, as they say, 'stopped a train'.

"Thanks, and thanks for getting my bag out and some clothes together."

"Sure, and how about a big hug for your long-suffering wife?" She smiled as I opened my arms.

"By the way, I'm packing Mark's term paper in with your things. You haven't read it yet and it's really good. He got an A. Give you something to do at night – keep you out of trouble." She laughed. "Keep your mind off that pretty young NSA gal."

"He wrote it on Scotland, didn't he?" I said, ignoring her innuendo and sly grin.

"Yes, all about our driving trip from Morocco and our time in Scotland. He titled it, "My life in Scotland.""

"Maybe he should be a writer rather than enlist in the Navy?"

"No, I think he wants to follow in his dad's footsteps, anyway, I need to finish this if you're flying away in the morning."

"Wish you could come along."

She stepped back and smiled. "And who would watch the kids? Now, what is it you need to do?"

"I need to call Andy Hetzel and hope he knows how to get in touch with Woody Floyd."

She gave me a puzzled look. "Andy … oh yeah, we got a card from them at Christmas. I think I saved it. Hold on … you can pick out your shirts while I look for the card."

"Do you remember where the card came from?"

"Somewhere in Delaware, Bell something."

"That's right, Bellefonte. Makes sense, it's close to Bethesda where Winslow said Andy was working as corpsman."

"You probably should try to reach him before we eat dinner; it's close to seven in the East."

They'd had showers after returning to the Plum Tree and both changed into casual clothes for the evening. For dinner Jennings suggested something other than the Bee Hive so they'd driven east to Elma and now sat across from each other looking over the Rusty Tractor's menu.

Gerri Jennings glanced over the top of hers. "What time's our flight?"

"The Lear lands at Bowerman Field in Hoquiam at nine," Spence answered.

"What about Seattle's car?"

"The NSA office will arrange for someone to pick it up."

"So we need to be at Herschel's at … ah what, eight?"

"I told him seven-thirty, just to make sure."

She looked back at the menu. *He looks a lot younger in jeans and a polo shirt. Cleans up pretty nice, too. Darn, why does he have to be so good looking?*

"The strip steak looks good," he said, all the time thinking, *Watch it Spence* – and, *Damn, she looks fantastic in those tan slacks and white blouse.* That was the problem, he was watching, and he couldn't seem to divert his eyes and focus on anything but her, let alone a menu.

"Hope he can get a hold of this Andy fellow and get a phone number for Woody Floyd … ah, here comes the waitress," she said, blushing when she realized he'd been staring at her, and not the menu.

They both ordered the 8-ounce sirloin strip and when asked opted for a glass of wine – both Merlot.

"Before she gets back with the wine, I thought this might help," she pulled a folded sheet of stationery from her purse and handed it to him. "I made it up before we left the motel."

Winslow unfolded the sheet and studied it. "This is great, puts it all in perspective – I was really getting mixed up, thanks. We should add the dates they were there, too."

Common Service Locales

	HI	PHIL	JAPAN	MORC	IM BCH	GUAM	FT MEADE	SCOT
Floyd	x	x			x			
Collins					x	x	x	
Chief	x		x	x	x		x	
O'Brien	x	x			x		x	
Payne	x	x	x	x	x	x	x	x

She answered on the fourth ring. "Hello."

"Hello, this is Herschel Payne, is this Ruth Hetzel?"

"Yes ... oh, Chief Payne, how nice."

"Yes, it's been a while – Barbara says hello, too. Listen, is Andy there?"

"No, I'm sorry you missed him, he's on nights at the hospital. Let's see ...he gets off at seven, usually home for breakfast about eight. Is it something I can help with?"

"Maybe, I'm trying to get a hold of Woody … Woody Floyd, and I thought Andy may know where he is."

"I know he talked to him recently, I … I'm pretty sure he's in the DC area because Andy and some of his other buddies helped him move last month."

I did a quick calculation, eight there, five here, the plane leaves at about nine, if I call before they pick me up … "Ruth, would you tell Andy I'll call about ten your time. It's really important that I talk to Woody."

"Can he call you?"

"Sure if it's before ten-thirty, I'm leaving for a …yeah, he can try that, and Ruth, again sorry to bother you so late."

Part Two

Trained to another use,
We march with colours furled,
Only concerned when Death breaks loose
On a front of half a world.
Only for General Death
The Yellow Flag may fly,
While we take post beneath –
That is the place for a spy.
Where Plague has spread his pinions over
    Nations and Dominions –
Then will be work for a spy!

Rudyard Kipling

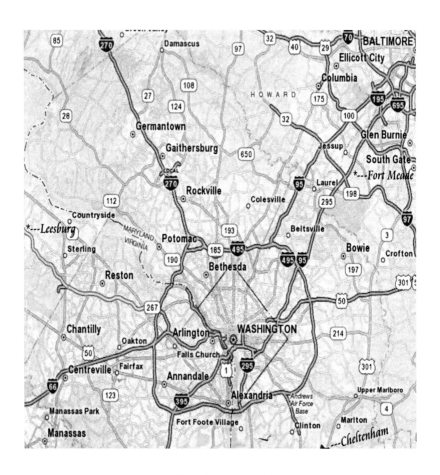

Greater Washington D.C. area

Fifteen

When I was a teenager the offshore landing field in Hoquiam, Washington was called Moon Island Airport. During my senior year at Elma High School the airport was renamed Bowerman Field after Robert Bowerman, a local veteran who'd been a fighter pilot during World War II and had worked hard to promote the airport. The airport was upgraded during the 60's and early 70's, eventually taken over by the Port of Grays Harbor, and today is coastal Washington's only jet-capable airport.

I had only flown a few times during my hitch in the Navy, mostly in what we called "prop-jobbers" like the DC-3 and certainly never in someone's private jet. The sight of the gleaming silver Lear jet parked on the tarmac near Bowerman's small terminal brought home once again the seriousness of the situation I found myself in the midst of. Winslow had already told me that NSA had a small fleet of Lear's, most were model 24D, a two-engine, eight passenger version of the jet. He'd added that this particular plane could climb to forty-two thousand feet in three minutes – not exactly a comforting thought to an already nervous ground pounder.

Add to that the towering cumulonimbus clouds over the Pacific, usually signaling an approaching storm, didn't help belie my fears.

"Will I have time to try and reach Andy again?" I asked. He hadn't called and I'd gotten no answer when I twice tried from home.

Winslow checked his watch, as the Plymouth pulled next to a nearby hangar. "You should have and there's got to be a phone in that hangar. You still have the phone card I gave you?"

"Yes."

"All right, you go call. Gerri and I will get things loaded … ah, here come the pilots. You've got about fifteen minutes."

The payphone hung on the wall next to a metal work bench piled high with various parts. I lifted the receiver. "Oh nice," I said out loud, looking around for a cloth to wipe off the grease so I didn't get it all over my freshly-ironed shirt sleeve or Winslow's credit card.

"Here we go." *One, two, three, four ...*

"Hello."

"Andy, finally. This is Hersch Payne."

"Figured it might be. Listen, I'm sorry, had a couple of last minute emergencies. Anymore nights like that and my black hair will turn even grayer. Ruth said you needed to get a hold of Woody."

"Yeah, hope you can help."

"He lives in an apartment in Mount Pleasant. Don't know if he's there now, but here's the phone number."

I copied the number. "Thanks again, Andy. I don't have much time before I leave, but say, I'll be in DC for a few days, and maybe we can get together."

"You're here now, I thought Ruth said you were at home in …"

"I am, but I'm flying out in a few minutes."

"For DC, wow, it must be important. Ruth said you sounded stressed out. What's the big deal?"

"Nothing for you to worry about, ah … *now what the hell do I say,* just some stuff that goes back a few years."

"Spy stuff, I bet. You old crypto guys must be having a reunion?"

"Why, no, why would you say that." *Now I've stuck my foot in it*, I thought.

"Oh, I was talking to Mick O'Brien today who said he'd been told to report to Fort Meade, and that he'd gotten a call from Russ Collins who also had been told to report there tomorrow. Now you're asking about Woody and are on your way here, too. Sounds like old spy stuff to me." He laughed.

"No, no, nothing that sinister … Andy, I've got to go. Thanks for the info., I'll give you a call when I can and maybe we can have lunch."

"Do you need a ride from Dulles?"

"Thanks, but no, we're going into Leesburg." *Damn I'm saying too much.*

After a long pause. "Okay, have a safe trip."

"Hello?"

"Woody, this is Hersch, long time no see, huh?"

"Hersch, I'll be damned. Where are you?"

"In Hoquiam, it's near my house in Montesano. I'm at an airport getting ready to fly to DC, courtesy of Uncle Sam."

"You're shittin me – c'mon Hersch we've known each other too long, what's this about?"

I tried to remember exactly what Winslow had told me to say. "I know you're retired like I am, but they need some experienced crypto guys like us to be part of a special team to help out during the meeting next week in Helsinki, Finland."

"I've been reading about that, I guess President Ford, Kissinger and the whole DC gang is going, but hey, they've got lots of young studs. So, why you and I?"

Winslow was walking my way and I could hear the sound of the jet's engines warming up.

"Woody, if you can meet me in the lobby of the main NSA conference hall at," I looked at Winslow, who held up six fingers, "at six today, I'll explain more, okay? Trust me."

"Guess I can, but this sounds sort of fishy …"

"There'll be a visitor's badge waiting for you at the gate."

"All right, six it is. But Hersch, I'll be there for you, not that bunch of white college boys."

I hung up the receiver. "I feel like a rat."

Winslow shook his head slowly. "Goes with the territory. Sorry but remember, he could be our mole. C'mon, the plane's ready to go."

Sixteen

My guts felt like they were going to pop out of my mouth and my rear end felt like it was being pile-driven through the seat – we were going straight up, and up and about the time I couldn't have held back a scream much longer, we leveled off.

Winslow glanced my way. "See, I told you. Quite a ride! These jet jockeys are real cowboys, ex Navy, most of 'em."

Jennings reached across, touching my hand. "I don't like it either."

A few minutes at cruising altitude and I realized I hadn't had time to use the toilet before we took off, lucky I didn't wet my pants on our climb. I looked around. She must have guessed.

"Toilet's behind that partition," she pointed to the rear. "Take your time, we went before takeoff. Oh, and Spence said we'd go over a few things at ten, so relax when you get back to your seat."

Returning to my seat I closed my eyes and chuckled quietly to myself. The incident with the toilet had reminded me of a time when I was ten and my brother Larry and I were sent to live with the Borden family at their ranch up the Satsop River.

That first night Larry and I were shown the house and where we were going to sleep. It was a school night, so Grandma Borden said we should be getting to bed soon so we could get up for school in the morning. She then told me to "go out and look at the moon." I thought it was a bit silly, but did it anyway. It so happened it was a clear night and the moon was brilliantly full. When I came back in and she asked me if I'd "looked at the moon" I said "sure", and commented on how bright and beautiful it was. She handed her grandson Sunny a lantern, and Larry and I followed him upstairs to the room we would share.

Not long after we got upstairs, I told Sunny I needed to "go pee." He said, "Didn't you go look at the moon?" I said, "Sure I did, but what's that got to do with taking a pee?" He replied, "That's just a saying she uses to tell us guys to go outside and pee. You look at the moon while you're doing it. Anyway, I keep a slop jar underneath my bed, go ahead and use it." That had been my introduction to the Borden family.

"There's coffee and donuts up forward, if you want, Hersch," Jennings said, bringing me out of my reminiscence.

"Thanks, I'm not sure my stomach is ready."

"C'mon anyway, Spence wants to get started."

I'd been in small aircraft before, but never at forty-two thousand feet and speeds well over Mach 1. It was amazing how quiet it was and I only had to slightly crouch walking down the aisle to where Winslow sat. I took the empty seat opposite him.

"Gerri said you were ready to get going."

"I am, here, take a look at this."

The heading on the single sheet of paper said, "Plum Tree Motel" and on the stationery someone had drawn a chart, horizontally across the top were the names of the duty stations where I'd served, vertically the names of Woody, Chief, Russ, Mick, and myself.

"So, is it accurate as far as you remember?"

"Yeah, but I know some of them were stationed at these places when I wasn't there."

"We know that, but for now I just want to make sure this much is correct."

Jennings took the aisle seat across from me. "The next step is to add the applicable dates and then the events where we know the mole leaked info to his contact at the embassy."

"Should help us narrow down the list even more," Winslow said. "The chart was Gerri's idea, by the way."

Jennings rose slightly and took a bow. "So, Hersch, let's go back over my notes and fill in some blanks. We've got a couple more hours and we also need to review our plan for tomorrow."

"Don't forget I'm meeting Woody tonight."

"Yeah, we need to factor that in too," she said.

Because it was a Sunday, our driver said it would take less than an hour to drive the 55 miles to Fort Meade whereas on a weekday just the route over Highway 267 to the DC belt exchange could be that long. The clock on the Ford's dash said four-twenty-one.

"We're cutting it close," I said to no one in particular.

"We'll be fine," Winslow said from the front seat. "Any questions on what you're going to say to Woody."

"I guess not – we've gone over it enough."

"Don't forget, we'll be in the next room, so if you need help, take a break, get him some coffee or something, and come next door."

"You'll be able to see us too, won't you?"

"Yeah, and we'll be taping the interview."

Seventeen

The lobby of the NSA conference hall had changed significantly since I'd last been there. The '60s era lightly painted walls, mahogany molding, tiled floor and sparseness of windows had been replaced with white-washed concrete walls accented with aluminum molding flowing down to oyster-gray marble floors. Where once had been an exterior wall with three small windows was now a thirty foot seamless sheet of glass. What light remained at 5:45 p.m. poured through the floor to ceiling pane illuminating the lone figure sitting on a bench to the right of the reception counter.

Woody Floyd had put on a few pounds since I'd last seen him twelve years earlier, but other than a few signs of graying in his curly raven-black hair, he looked much the same. He snuffed out his cigarette and rose to greet me.

"You don't look a lot different, Hersch, maybe a bit thicker in the gut and a little less hair."

"I was thinking the same about you." I accepted his strong grip. "Thanks for coming."

"Sure, hope I can help you and as I said, it's for you, not those bastards that forced me out. I had almost twenty-five years, could still work circles around the new breed of hotshots."

"Bet you could, Woody. I sure remember those times in Japan and at San Miguel when you decoded the message from that trapped Cuban ship. You were fast."

"Still am, but twenty-five years counts for shit when you fail the damned Master Chief test three times."

"Hey, at least you got to Senior Chief. I never was a good test-taker. Anyway, I really appreciate you coming." I turned and walked to the lone reception desk attendant.

"I'm Herschel Payne," I said, handing him the documents Winslow had given me before he and Jennings had left me off and driven to the rear of the building. "I believe there's a room reserved for Mr. Floyd and I."

The young man behind the counter sporting what looked to be a freshly-cut flattop perused the three pages quickly, as if he'd already seen them, nodded and handed me a clip-on visitor's badge similar to the one worn by Woody.

"You're in room 3-B, down that corridor, second room on the left," he said, pointing towards the opening to my right.

To say that Room 3-B was austere would have been an understatement. With the exception of an eight-foot long wooden table and eight upholstered chairs, the lodge-style room was devoid of any adornments – no pictures on the walls, no blackboard or easel, no cabinets, definitely no ashtrays, and the only illumination was provided by six overhead track lights. A solitary American flag stood in the right corner. A black buttonless telephone lay on the table.

"Once again, our government has spared no expense," Woody said.

"They're saving the taxpayers money. Reminds me of that time in the Philippines when they started rationing the toilet paper at the base." I glanced around the room again, wondering where the cameras were hidden.

Woody must have read my mind. "They probably got bugs in every nook and cranny, and cameras in the light fixtures."

"I doubt that, but who knows, it's a different world from when swabbies like you and I signed on." I pulled out one of the chairs and motioned to the one opposite.

"Looks like you're getting serious – but, I guess that's why you asked me to come. Okay, let's have it. I've already figured that business about needing me for a special project is a load of crap," he said aloud and in a tone as if he were speaking for a recording session.

"Not completely, NSA does need some help with the message flow from Helsinki, but you're right, of course, that's not the main reason."

"I knew it, just another Jim Crow scheme in the making."

"Shit, Woody, get serious, we need your help." I shook my head. "You remember when we were on the *Yorktown* and handling all those messages about Operation Ivory Coast?"

"Yeah, ah …that was in '66."

"Do you remember that the rebels got support from Cuba, and when we tried to help Mumbata's Army, Che Guevara seemed to know every step we took and eventually the rebels overran the government troops?"

"I do for sure. We could never figure out how Che seemed always to be one step ahead."

"Well, he was getting his information from the North Koreans."

"What? C'mon, how could that be?"

I looked him straight in the eyes. "Someone in our team was giving all the Operation Ivory Coast communications to a contact at the Korean embassy in DC and this person was somehow getting the info to Cuba."

Woody's eyes almost popped out of his head and he slowly shook his head. "You mean we had a mole, a spy in our CT bunch."

He didn't ask it as a question, but rather as a conclusion.

"The operative word is 'has' not 'had'."

"I'll be a son-of-a-bitch!"

"NSA first thought it could have been me – I had all the crypto skills, was working the Ivory Coast Op and had been around when similar leaks had taken place, in fact I seem to have been on station the majority of the other times."

"How many 'other times'?"

"At least a couple dozen that NSA knows of and a current one that puts President Ford and his upcoming mission to Finland in jeopardy …"

Woody sat quietly. "How did NSA find out about all this?"

"A North Korean agent defected and told us. He knows the code name of the mole, 'Cronus', but doesn't know his identity."

"Okay, so why …oh, I get it, you think I'm a candidate, but I've been out of …"

"I know, but here's the thing, NSA thinks the mole is one of three people: Chief Callgrove, Mick O'Brien, or Russ Collins."

"Not me?"

"No." I hated lying to a man who'd been and I hoped still was a good friend, but I continued to follow the script Winslow and Jennings had provided. "We need your help in finding out which of the three it is. And, there's something else you should know, NSA has narrowed down the spy list at the Korean embassy and should be arresting Cronus's contact soon."

I could tell Woody was relaxing, and I needed a break. "You still smoke I see."

"Yeah, and I could use something to drink too – water that is, for now."

"Let's do it then, and I'll explain how you can help."

The camera in the flagpole's ball ornament in room 3-B provided an excellent picture for Winslow and Jennings, just as the tiny mike under the table transmitted a clear conversation to their earphones and the tape recorder in room 3-C.

They watched as Herschel and Woody left the room. "He did a good job," Winslow said.

"You think Floyd believed him?"

"I think so, but we'll see what happens."

"You think if Floyd's the mole he'll warn his contact at the embassy?" Jennings asked.

"That's the idea and if all goes as planned we'll also find out whom the bugger is."

"I'm still not clear … I …"

"Okay," Winslow said, "I'll go over it again. Herschel is going to let slip to each guy the new schedule for President Ford's meeting with President Kekkonen at his private residence in Helsinki, but here's the tricky part … oops, they're back, more later."

"Sounds too simple to me," she said in a whisper.

"Gerri, they can't hear us."

Eighteen

"So I'm joining the others for a briefing here, tomorrow at 1300 hours?" Woody asked me. "Guess I should say one o'clock now that I'm a civilian. It's hard to break old habits."

"Yes, one p.m. There will actually be eight of us, including Russ, Chief and Mick who will make up the communications support group for Helsinki."

"For real? I thought this whole thing was a ruse."

"Yes, for real, but all the time I want you to help me keep an eye on those three."

I'd known Woody long enough to tell by his expression he was struggling with seeing how his observations could help, and was reluctant to ask about it – maybe he could sense my own doubts about the feasibility of the scheme or that I was holding something back. It reminded me of the time in Hawaii when he'd asked me several times what was wrong and I'd told him "nothing" yet I was agonizing over the news of my father's worsening health.

That morning I'd received a telegram from the Red Cross asking me to call home. I found out my dad had a tumor on his lower spine. Working with the Red Cross and my CO, I was able to get emergency leave and arrange a flight the next afternoon from Honolulu to Travis Air Force Base near San Francisco and luckily catch a hop to Payne Field in Everett.

In the midst of all the scheduling I realized I was in charge of the evening watch – I had eight men on my watch section. That's when I knew it was time to fess up to Woody. He'd not hesitated in his decision, and other than a snide remark about his being right that something was wrong, doubled up and covered both his and my watch section while I was gone.

I jumped as the phone rang. "Hello." I knew it was Winslow in the next room as it had been prearranged, but I still was startled by the suddenness of it.

"Yes sir, and that is the final schedule?" I paused, feigning surprise and continued listening. "All right, I understand," I said, hanging up.

Woody's eyebrows furrowed into a vee shape.

"That was my contact for this little op … he said they've firmed up Ford's itinerary in Helsinki and reminded me how important our team's work will be. He'll brief us in more detail tomorrow. It does sound like they've covered all the bases right down to Ford's meeting with Kekkonen at his residence; get this, not at eight or eight-thirty, but eight-fifteen."

Woody pushed back his chair. "Maybe they'll serve him something to eat – a lot more than they do in this dump."

I looked at my watch. "Man, it is way past dinner time, sorry. If you want to get a bite, I think we're finished for today – we'll put it on NSA's tab along with your hotel bill."

"Thanks, but I haven't seen Andy in a coon's age and he and I are meeting at The Bombay Club at seven … ah, want to join us?"

"No, but thanks, I've got a lot to do before our meeting tomorrow, I'll catch a bite at my hotel. Say hi to Andy, and remember, all we've been talking about is hush, hush."

Winslow and Jennings were waiting for me when I returned from walking Woody to his car.

"So, what do you think?"

"What do you mean, 'what do I think'? You two heard the whole thing," I said, answering Winslow. "Do you mean do I think he's the mole, or do I think he bought it?"

Winslow realized from my tone I was not a happy camper. "Sorry, I know that wasn't easy. I meant primarily, do you think he bought our story – if he is the mole, hopefully we'll know by this time tomorrow."

"All right, I'm just worn to a frazzle and not looking forward to repeating this three times in the morning."

"We understand," said Jennings, "we'll all go for dinner if you want or we'll take you back to the Holiday Inn. It's up to you, we're tired too. It's been a long day."

"The Holiday, I'll grab something there and hit the sack. Let's see, the meeting with Russ is at eight, so you'll pick me up at …"

"We'll meet you for breakfast at six," Winslow said.

Their assigned driver, who might as well have been mute for all the talking he did, pulled away from the curb and headed down C Street SW. They'd not discussed their own plans beyond checking into the Ramada in College Park. Jacob Harding had felt it best his two agents remain in DC, but staying at the same hotel as Herschel Payne had not been deemed wise. The car turned again and the top of the brightly lit Washington Monument came into view.

"I never get over the sight of that." She yawned. "Oops, sorry, bed will feel good – I'm tired even though it's only around five p.m. west coast time," Gerri said, choking off another yawn.

"Me too, I'm beat. We should be there in a few minutes, how about we check in and meet for a late dinner and discuss what's on for tomorrow."

"Sounds good," she answered, but as she spoke wondered whether it really was a good idea. She had little doubt that the attraction she felt for him was mutual. *Two single people obviously attracted to one another, a couple drinks, a secluded hotel – a recipe for disaster perhaps... a career-ender?* "Yes, that sounds fine."

Nineteen

I'm really not feeling fine, or "fit as a fiddle" like my Aunt Lillie used to say. Whether it is the hurriedly devoured tuna salad sandwich that rested undigested in my stomach, the overly hard hotel bed-pillow or the events of the day – which by themselves would be enough to create acidity – I couldn't get to sleep. The afternoon's recollections of the time of my dad's illness just wouldn't go away. *Man, almost ten years ago.*

I'd ended up spending six weeks in Washington State, some quality time with my dad in Aberdeen, but mostly unpleasant memories regarding the rest of my family.

I heard that my stepfather Oscar had been miffed about "upsetting his routine" but at my mother's insistence had finally agreed and picked me up at Payne Field in Everett. My first night's sleeping accommodations were in a dirty pickup camper and the only ground transportation provided for me to get to the hospital was an old, barely running International pickup. I did spend time with my brother Larry, who despite being estranged from our dad due to his dislike of our stepmother Pearl, visited the hospital a few times. I also managed to visit some high school chums in Moses Lake, but Dad's quickly-spreading cancer cast an ever-present pall over everything.

Dad never left the hospital. About a month after I returned to Hawaii my Aunt Lillie called to tell me he had passed away.

Exhaustion finally ruled and somewhere around eleven I drifted off.

Master Chief Petty Officer Russell Collins arrived at the NSA conference center precisely at eight AM in full dress uniform.

Spence, Gerri and I had reviewed the strategy over breakfast and they were now ensconced in room 3-C. I rose from the lobby bench and walked to greet my old Navy buddy.

"Hersch, you son-of-a gun, good to see you," he said, the hard-to-forget, captivating smile framing his handsome face. "Great to see they still need some of the old CT gang. Jeez, what's it been," he paused, "at least six or seven years."

"Seven, I think since Norfolk."

"Ah, don't remind me about that fiasco, never could get my hands to work fast enough to repair those damned crypto machines, let alone remember the names of all the parts."

I nodded, walked to the reception desk and retrieved his badge. "They already cleared you through at the gate, but you'll need this while you're here. C'mon, we're going to a room down that hallway, and by the way, thanks for coming."

He clipped on the ID badge. "Didn't have a choice did I?" Russ laughed. "It was a bit of a downer leaving the crystal clear waters and soothing breezes of Hawaii for a hot and humid DC, but here I am, always ready to serve." He gave me a hard pat and chuckled.

"Speaking of clear waters, remember the fun we had scuba diving in Guam? You always lied about those big bubbles – said they were from your faulty regulator, but we all knew those were farts – whew, did those ever muck up the water and the air." Russ laughed loudly; while I'm sure my face turned a brilliant crimson red.

Fifteen minutes later, Russ sat still in his chair. His cavalier demeanor abandoned, his eyes lowered. I'd finished the story given to Woody ten hours earlier.

"Woody, Mick or Chief, a spy – no I can't believe it, there's got to be a mistake. Christ, Woody's not even in the Navy any more. And this CT 'team' for Helsinki is for real, but I'm still supposed to keep watch on my lifelong friends to see if they do anything suspicious – this is for the birds, Hersch. Son-of-a-bitch, it's like a Greek tragedy."

The phone rang. As I reached for the receiver, I thought, *Bruce would just love this playacting – hope I'm as good an actor as he is.*

"Hello. Yes this is Payne. Yes sir!" As before, I pretended to be listening intently. "I understand. Yes this afternoon. Okay, see you then."

Without waiting for a question, I looked at Russ. "That was the head of this op, making sure everything is set for this afternoon. Man, you wouldn't believe the detail in the plans for Helsinki – crazy!"

"How so?"

"The schedule for Ford's visit to Kekkonen's place next week, he'll arrive at nine-fifteen, not nine or nine-thirty, but nine-fifteen. Probably some young spook's idea, anyway, sorry for the interruption."

"No problem. It sounds like everything's under control and on schedule, not like it was for you and me back on Guam."

"How's that?"

"You know," Russ said, "never having any good transportation to and from Camp Weitek and always having to hitch a ride."

"Yeah." I sensed as he said this that in his own fashion he was making reference to the night in Agana when I'd missed the last bus. He and I seemed to have had a strained relationship after that.

Then almost as another effort to belie my recollections of the "gay" incident, he said, "By the way, my wife says hello."

"Thanks, bet she's not happy about you being gone – just like mine."

He smiled. "So what next?"

"For now that's it. The team briefing is at one, as I said. If you want to talk with me personally, here's where I'm staying." I handed him a piece of the hotel stationery. "And remember, not a word of this to anyone." I rose and reached across to shake his hand. "C'mon, I'll walk you out a side door; it's closer to the parking lot."

The Cronus Cypher

The hallway clock showed it was 8:43. *Whew, not a minute too soon.*

Twenty

Mick O'Brien was late.

I knocked on room 3-C's door. "What do you think, Spence?"

"We heard there's a big pile-up on the freeway, cars backed up all the way to Cheltenham," Winslow said. "Be patient, we've still got some leeway."

My loner Motorola pager vibrated. "That's probably him."

Mick hadn't lost his boyish good looks – the red hairline had receded, and the unbuttoned jacket revealed a paunch above his belt, but he still had a youthful sparkle in his eyes and a bounce in his step. If it had been St. Patrick's Day you'd have expected him to launch into a chorus of "Danny Boy".

"Faith and begorra it's me ole buddy Hersch!"

He shook my hand then pulled me into a bear hug.

"Sorry I'm late, damn DC traffic. Could a run out of gas."

"That's okay, you're here and that's what counts." I handed him the NSA visitor's badge. "You'll need this."

"I'll take it, but I'm working at Fort Meade now, got my own badge." He looked around. "Haven't been in this old building for a while, like what they've done. So, what's up?

From what my orders said, I'm to be part of some special ops team."

"Yes, you are."

"So, they pulled you out of retirement to head this thing up?"

"Why don't we go to the conference room and I'll explain the whole shebang."

"**Y**ou know Hersch, this reminds me of that time in the Philippines when if a war had broken out, we were going to be evacuated by sub and the families were going to have to fend for themselves in the jungle. Typical navy bullshit. My God, spying on my friends, toss 'm to the wolves."

I nodded and started to speak, but Mick was just warming up.

"I can just see that officer telling us that if the blockade was unsuccessful and war was declared, the families were on their own. I know you were really concerned about Barbara and your two kids. Man, what gall ..."

"Mick, this is different, the President's safety is at stake," I offered when he finally took a breath.

"I suppose. Okay, so we meet this afternoon at 1300 hours, and from that point on I'm going to watch Woody, Chief and Russ and report to you any suspicious activity. Damn it, one of our Navy buddies is a spy, I still don't believe it."

"Yes, but remember, we are still going to support the Helsinki Conference."

"Yeah ..."

The phone rang. "Yes, I see, okay. Yes, I understand." Bruce would have been proud. I shook my head and grimaced "That's fine, yes I'll see you at 1300 hours."

As Russ had done, Mick looked at me questionably.

"Talk about ridiculous," I said, "now they're changing the time for President Ford's meeting next week with Kekkonen, and, you won't believe this, instead of meeting at ten or ten-thirty, they're going to meet precisely at ten-fifteen. Fifteen after! Some newbie's idea, I bet." I took a quick peek at my watch. *Quarter of.*

"That's for sure … same ole NSA," he said.

"Mick, thanks again and I know this is a lot to fathom. You've got a couple of hours before the briefing. I'd have lunch with you, but I need to tie up a few loose ends." Remember, not a word to Woody and the others."

As I had done before, I led one of my friends, a possible enemy agent, down the hallway to the side exit.

The ten o'clock appointment was the one I dreaded the most. Of all the suspects, Chief Callgrove was the one I'd served with most recently and by far the one man who epitomized the American dream. Born into poverty, withstood the prejudices of discrimination, overcame a serious drinking problem, was loyal to a fault and had risen to the highest rating for an enlisted man in the Navy.

"How was the flight?" He looked surprised to see me – more than the others did.

"C'mon Hersch, you know I hate flying, but not too bad. Short layover in Denver, then direct to Dulles – smooth all the way. Worst thing about it was I couldn't have a cigar."

"Still smoke those god-awful smelly things, huh?"

"Only thing that keeps me going sometimes, a good Montecristo, but NSA didn't invite me here for old times' sake, what's the deal – you're retired, right?"

"I am, but NSA asked me to coordinate the op and, well, I couldn't think of anyone else I'd rather have working with me."

"You mean an old Indian like me still has something to offer?"

"Chief, they wouldn't have you teaching at Imperial Beach if they didn't think you did." I reached into my pocket and handed him an ID badge. "You'll need this for the next several days. I've got a room where we can talk, c'mon."

We took opposite seats in room 3-B and without preamble, I began.

Charles Dickens had his "Twice Told Tales"; I had my thrice plus one told tale. Chief's reaction was much the same as the others. Not exactly an Oscar winning performance but apparently good enough.

"This is bullshit, you know; Russ Collins, Mick O'Brien or Woody Floyd a spy – somebody at NSA has their head up you know where!"

"Trust me, Chief, sad to say, but true."

"I trust you, but you know this is guilty without trial – not until proven guilty, it reminds me of what you told me happened with your wife in Morocco while we were on the *Galveston* in '69."

"What was that?"

"Lose'n a bit of the old recall, huh?" He chuckled. "Remember they caught some Moroccan guy trying to steal your car and a guard that was protecting another neighbor spotted him. I can't recall why he was there… ah, anyway, the guard handcuffed and took the guy away while Barbara watched. Then Barbara had to go to the police station and identify him, but the guy's face was so swollen and bloody, she couldn't. They'd beat the guy to a pulp – punishment before any kind of trial – guilty – that's what I mean."

"Yeah, I see your point. The guard, as I remember now, was protecting some important Algerian exile and his family. Okay, point well taken, but regardless, one of our friends is guilty of spying. I admit it's stupid, but that's what the evidence shows."

On cue, the phone rang.

I went through the same routine as before.

"Talk about stupid." I returned the receiver to its cradle with a bang.

"What's that?"

"Oh, they just revised President Ford's Helsinki schedule for the umpteenth time and his meeting next week with President Kekkonen is set for eleven-fifteen, not eleven-thirty or eleven, but fifteen after. Probably some new NSA spook's idea."

"Yup, that's why I'm looking forward to getting out next year."

"They'll miss you, Chief."

"Maybe, maybe not. Say, if the briefing is at 1300, shouldn't we be wrapping this up."

"Yeah, listen, I can't join you for lunch, but I'll see you in an hour. The cafeteria should be open, it's on the second floor, and remember if you see any of the guys, don't mention our conversation."

"Okay, oh, and by the way, the room at the Sheraton is nice, first class."

After walking Chief to the elevator, I went down the hallway to find Winslow and Jennings standing outside room 3-C.

"Good job, Hersch. If everything goes according to plan, we should know something later today," Winslow said.

I looked at him and shook my head. "Did you hear anything in the four conversations that narrows down the list?"

"Not for sure. Gerri thinks it's between Woody and Mick O'Brien, but I lean towards Collins or Callgrove. Either way, we've got the Korean embassy wired to the hilt so we'll keep our fingers crossed – it's a simple plan, but sometimes simple is best. We've got some time before Harding's briefing, so let's go over everything again. I've got some sandwiches coming from the cafeteria. There's also some ground I want to cover on Morocco and Chief Callgrove before the briefing."

I hesitated. "What about the mole's supposed contact at the Seattle legation, maybe the mole will contact him or her instead?"

"I doubt it, but we've got that covered, too. Don't worry. Oh, here comes our lunch."

Twenty-One

I was hungrier than I realized and woofed down the ham and cheese sandwich in short order. Spence and Gerri appeared equally famished and only the sounds of smacking lips were heard for several minutes. Maybe we were just talked out, I know I was.

I failed at holding back a burp – *always happens when I eat too fast.*

"Oops, sorry."

"That's okay, it's a compliment you enjoyed your food in some countries," Spence said. "Don't know whether NSA cafeteria food counts, though."

I nodded and cleared my throat. "You said there was 'some ground to cover' on Chief, having something to do with Morocco. I thought we'd pretty well hashed that over before we left Montesano?"

"Yeah, we did as far as your time with him in '69, but Harding's guys came up with another angle involving 1958, shortly after his Captain's Mast."

The Cronus Cypher

"When did you get that information?"

"It was given to us while you were interviewing Callgrove."

Spence glanced Gerri's way. "Gerri, you take it from here."

"You remember, Hersch, when we asked you about Bernon Mitchell and William Martin?"

I nodded.

She continued. "Well, in 1958 Mitchell was sent to Rabat to program the System-V equipment for the U-2."

"I never knew they had U-2's at Rabat?"

"Yes, we were using Rabat for training the pilots in operating the new eavesdropping equipment for the Green Hornet missions."

"Okay, I knew about the U-2 Green Hornet missions, but what's that got to do with Chief?"

"The frequency of the System-V eavesdropping equipment was known by only a few and its programmer, Mitchell. We can't prove beyond a shadow of a doubt that Bernon Mitchell and Chief Callgrove worked together, or even saw each other in '58, but it has come to light, that the Soviets were given the frequencies by the North Koreans in 1960."

"So, I don't see …"

"Francis Gary Powers' ill-fated mission was not only to photograph the Soviet's missile test range but to eavesdrop and record their radar signals for NSA. The Soviets locked on to his eavesdropping equipment frequency and brought him down with one of their SA-2 missiles. Without the frequency, they'd of had no chance to hit him at his altitude."

"But if Chief was the mole and had the frequency data, why wait for almost two years to pass it on to the North Koreans?"

"That's the 64-dollar question, but when Chief told you he never knew Mitchell, it's hard to believe they didn't come in contact with each other at Rabat in '58."

"How about Mick. Remember, I said that he knew Martin. Wouldn't he be just as much a suspect?"

"Good point, I'll tell Harding to check out that angle – I suppose Mitchell could have passed on the data to someone when he got back from Morocco, but the coincidence of Chief and Mitchell being at Rabat at the same time is still undeniable."

Spence looked at his watch. "We haven't got a lot of time left. Let's review what we know so far and kick around some ideas on what to do when and if our mole takes the bait."

Twenty-Two

Jacob Harding spent the first half hour of the briefing introducing the eight members of the team, defining their mission and why each of them had been selected. The team consisted of two Master Chief Petty Officers, four Senior Chiefs and two retired Chief's, all with extensive communications experience and specialists in cryptology. Harding would be the team leader, supported by Winslow. Agent Jennings was introduced as an observer and someone who would assist Harding and Winslow when required. No mention was made that she was an NSA profiler.

Most of the men in the room had served together, some multiple times, and had been amicably conversing with each other when Harding had entered the room followed by Winslow, Jennings and Herschel.

The team was divided into two groups, each to cover a twelve hour shift beginning in three days and lasting the length of the conference in Helsinki. Group I consisted of the following men: Chief, Russ, Woody, and Senior Chief Petty

Officer Barnett. This group would be supervised by Barnett; Herschel, Mick and two other men from Ft. Meade would make up the second group, supervised by Mick.

The balance of the afternoon would be spent learning the ciphers that would be used and the procedures for communicating with the men at the conference.

Harding passed a folder to each man that contained the information, however, not included was any mention of Ford's private meeting with Kekkonen.

"We'll train until four today and again on Wednesday. That should give an experienced bunch like you men time to prepare. We'll take Thursday off and begin our shifts on Friday at seven a.m. The advance group for the conference, including our NSA men arrives in Helsinki on Friday afternoon, then over the next several days the President and his staff and Secretary Kissinger arrive. The conference begins formal sessions on the following Tuesday – questions?"

During the balance of the afternoon, I tried to spend equal time with each man – it was "like old times" and if not for the dark cloud hanging over, it would have been one of my happiest days since retirement. At each short break, Chief, Woody, Mick, Russ and I naturally gravitated together, recalling many good times together. I couldn't keep from wondering how much if anything they'd discussed about our individual meetings earlier in the day, and for Woody, the day before. At a few minutes after four, Harding brought everyone together, told us dinner was on NSA and to get a good rest. Chief and Russ walked up to me.

"Hersch, Chief and I are going to the hotel, take a shower, grab some beers and then have dinner at the hotel. Do you want to join us?"

"Sure," I answered, "you're both staying at the Sheraton, right?" Knowing full well they were. "How about Mick and Woody?"

"Mick's going to his place and then meeting Woody, catch some brewskies and then hook up with us later," Russ offered.

"Sounds like a plan, I said, "as long as we can knock off early. Tomorrow's going to be a long day and I need to call Barb and the kids."

Cronus was finally alone. He and Hae-won had decided to start using a new code base this month and he was struggling to transcribe his message into the new cypher. Ki-woon in Seattle had wanted to continue using the Iliad, but Cronus and Zeus agreed with Hae-won and the Bible it was.

He looked up – The CBS Evening News had started. Walter Cronkite was a <u>must</u>, a ritual for him, so he lay down his pencil. The lead story had to do with the forthcoming conference in Finland. How timely, he thought. A few minutes wouldn't matter and maybe he needed a break – clear his head, then he could complete the message and get it off to Hae-won.

Cronkite always ended his broadcast the same way. "And that's the way it is."

The Cronus Cypher

It sure is. Back to work he thought and reopened his favorite book in his new Bible.

Twenty minutes later he'd finished the message and drove to a pay-phone near the hotel.

Cronus dialed Hae-won's number at the embassy.

She answered on the fifth ring. "Hello, this is Hae-won."

He hung up and dialed again. This time she picked up on the fourth ring. He counted to ten and with a handkerchief over his mouth said, "This is Cronus, message follows."

She counted silently to ten and said in Korean, "Chal ji-nae-ssŏ-yo" which meant "Good", indicating she was alone and to proceed.

He held the paper up to the light and began. "1221, 12222, 22222." Pause. "12222, 22111…"

After a long pause indicating he was done he said, "Cronus out," and hung up.

Cronus had never met Hae-won, but he'd covertly observed the attractive lady on several occasions. She had no idea who he was. He was being especially careful considering the defection of Sun, one of the reasons he'd lobbied to change the code base. He was doubly convinced that the CIA or NSA or both had put two-and-two together and as a precaution, had the Korean Embassy bugged. He was sure Sun had no idea of Cronus' identity or he would have been arrested by now, however he wasn't sure whether Sun knew that Hae-won was working for the North.

Once the date and time of Ford and Kekkonen's meeting had been transmitted to the operatives in Europe, his part in the operation was done. In fact he had been thinking for months

114

now it was time to stop – stop completely, 20 years – he'd been lucky, but the Feds were getting smarter, using more sophisticated methods. *I'll always hate them all for what they did.*

When he got to his car, he lit a cigarette and then held the paper with the message over the lighter's flame letting it drop into the gutter.

Mother would have been proud!

Twenty-Three

"It's like the time I had that huge boil on my butt."

"Herschel!"

"No, really, I feel like I'll burst any minute – this is really hard Barb. You remember how much pain I was in when I fell on that bus when we were going square dancing in San Miguel and I popped the sucker."

"Yes, how could I forget it. They could have heard you in Manila."

"Well, this is just as bad."

"I'm sorry, wish I was there."

"Me too. I am going out later with Russ and Chief, maybe Woody and Mick, too, so although it'll be awkward, it should be fun, like old times."

"Alright, but be sure and get some rest tonight. Love you, and call me tomorrow."

"Love you too, Angel. Give the kids a hug for me."

The Cronus Cypher

Muggsey's Tap Room and lounge in the Ramada was packed for a Monday night and they'd gotten the last two spaces at the end of the bar. Gerri Jennings gingerly sipped at her Foxsglove Chardonnay, but Spencer Winslow had drunk most of his vodka martini and between them they'd eaten all of the Brie and Brioche left on the happy hour table.

"It's almost seven and we haven't heard anything," Winslow said, disgustedly, "missed dinner, too."

"So, maybe we're wrong or else the mole didn't fall for our little charade."

He reached across and grasped her forearm. His touch was electric.

She didn't pull away, but gently placed her hand on top of his.

"I think I'll have another." He waved at the barmaid.

"You sure, you know I ..."

"Hold on – that's my pager." He removed the device from his pocket.

"Let's go to my room, this may be it."

"You go ahead, I'll sign the tab and be right up," she said.

By the time the elevator reached the first floor, Jennings was by his side. "Glad it was slow, you deserve to be there." He swayed slightly. "Oops, happy I didn't have another one."

As soon as they got in Winslow's room, he dialed nine and then the local number showing on the pager.

The number answered on the second ring. "This is Winslow. Okay, great. Yes. Yes, we can, we'll get Payne and be right there."

The Cronus Cypher

Director Jacob Harding and two of his staff were seated at a small conference table in Harding's office in the Information Assurance wing of NSA headquarters at Fort Meade when the guard ushered in Winslow, Jennings and I.

Harding rose and walked to me. "Chief Payne, thanks for coming and helping us, I know we've put you and your family under a lot of stress." He nodded at Winslow and Jennings. "Spence, Gerri, you too, it's been a long day, but I think we've finally got something."

With no mention of last names, Harding pointed at the two men still seated. "Frank and Stan here have been going over the message since we got it just before seven – they could use your help, Herschel."

I walked to the table and looked at the sheet of paper in front of Frank. On it were written a string of the numbers one and two, nothing else. The same numbers were written on a large pad of paper resting on an easel.

"Frank, play the tape," Harding said, "and listen closely to the voice."

I listened to the recording, – a monotonous voice droned on.

"Chief Payne, recognize anything, inflections, tone, anything?"

"No." I answered, as the voice droned on – "12222 21111 21111 …"

"Sounds to me like he's got something over his mouth," Jennings said when the tape recording ended. "Do you know who was at the other end?"

"Not positive, but of the three people that left the embassy after the call was received, two had access to the phone extension used, a female secretary, Hae-won and the Ambassador's aide, Mi-Song, so it's got to be one of them. We've always thought Cronus' contact was Mi-Song, but now, I'm not so sure. Anyway, we can deal with that later. Right now we need to decipher this message and see which of our men took the bait." Harding handed me a copy of the number one-two sequence. "What's your initial take?"

"Without any definitive breaks, it's hard to say – every once in a while, he does pause slightly, so I'd guess … wait awhile, it could be Morse code, the one a dit, the two a dah. Play the tape again, as slow as you can and see if you hear slight pauses."

"That makes sense," Winslow interjected, "these guys were all skilled at Morse code, even though it's not used much anymore, it fits."

I chuckled.

"What's so funny Herschel?" Winslow asked.

"Oh, I just was remembering big Jim Lane, the hired hand at Bignold's farm in Elma when I worked there during my senior year in high school. He told me that once you learned how to milk a cow, you never forgot – sorta like Morse code, except if you forget the code, you don't get kicked by an ornery Guernsey."

No one laughed, but Gerri smiled.

Frank rewound the tape.

Twenty-Four

"That's it!"

Three sheets of paper from the flip-chart lay discarded on the floor, but on our fourth try, we seemed to have agreement on the sequence of numbers.

1221 12222 22222 12222 22111 12222 21111 11112 11222
21111 12222 21111 21111

12222 21111 21111 12222 21111 12222 11222 21111
12222 11222 21111 11111 12222

21111 21111 21111 22221 12222 11222 22211 11122
12222 21111 12222 12222 22111

21111 22221 12222 22111 12222 21111 12222 12222
21111 21111 12222 21111 21111 21111 11111

The Cronus Cypher

"If this is right, I mean if the pauses are in the right spots, then except for the first set, the rest are all numbers, five digits," I said to the group and set the marker down.

"That would make sense, because the defector, Jon ta Sun, told us the received messages were always numbers – numbers that matched letters," Harding said.

I took a seat and turned to Harding. "What's the most recent code base, I mean do we know what they've been using to encrypt the numbers?"

"Homer's Iliad, according to Sun. They switch back and forth, Book One, then Three, and so forth," Agent Frank answered. "Sun told us that up to two years ago Cronus was using the Bible."

"How many books are there in the Iliad?" I asked.

"Twenty-four, but so far according to Sun, the mole's only used the first ten books."

I stood and walked back to the flip-chart. "If we assume you're correct, and he hasn't deviated, and assuming we've heard right and the first series has only four digits, then it's the letter 'P', followed by the number '10' which then could mean page ten of one of the books."

"But which book?" Winslow asked. "Plus that's a big assumption. If I was them and knew Sun had defected, I'd be changing my codes."

Harding rose and walked to the chart and stood next to me. "Okay, let's take a quick break and then we can put numbers to these series of dit-dahs. Maybe that will give us some hints where to go."

Often I do my best thinking in the shower or while sitting waiting for the bus – all of a sudden a thought pops into my mind or the answer to something I've been stewing over is revealed. As I walked out to have a smoke it was like all the neurons in my brain were firing at high speed. What was it? A distant memory? Something said in our discussion was triggering a thought, but I couldn't get it to the surface, the electrons were not aligned. *The Iliad ... hmm ...*

Russ and Chief waved at Woody and Mick when they entered the Sheraton's District Grill Bar.

"Over here," Chief said, standing so they could see him. "Where the hell have you guys been?"

"Don't blame me," Woody took forever to change, I must have sat in that lobby for fifteen minutes," Mick said.

"Hey, you weren't in the lobby the first time I went down."

"Where's Hersch, thought he was going to join us?" Woody asked, ignoring Mick's comment and taking a seat next to Russ.

"Don't know, but I could use another beer and you guys need to catch up."

"Is that right," Woody said. "Listen, I'm the only 'shellback' in this bunch of 'pollywogs'. If there's any catching up to do you'll soon be the ones to do it."

"Hey, Woody, you're not up-to-date," Russ said, giving Woody a shove. "I crossed the equator last year on the *Valcour*. I'm a full-fledged member of the Neptune Society, took my dive in the slop and kissed ole King Neptune's belly button, yes I did," referring to the traditional initiation ceremony for those crossing the equator for the first time.

"All right – let's drink. If Hersch shows he'll really have some catching up to do."

The clock on Harding's desk showed twenty minutes past nine, and we were no closer to an answer. The series of ones and twos, the dit-dahs, had been replaced by their Morse code equivalents: P,10. 17,164,26,166,166,161,26,12,65,166,69,128, 31,161,17,69,17,161,166,166 and 65.

"Now what?" Winslow set aside the large volumes of Homer's Iliad gotten earlier from the Smithsonian by Frank and Stan.

"Page ten in each of Homer's first ten books gets us nowhere. Four are blank, one has a drawing and on the others, if we assume the numbers are word positions and the beginnings of words, the results don't spell anything, just nonsense," Harding said. "This is a nightmare; we'll never figure it out."

"They could have switched to any of the 24 books – 'ten' could be page ten in any of them," I added. "One thing for sure though, we should be able to conclude that the numbers that are the same, that repeat, like 166 and 161 are the same word or letter."

"I agree," said Harding. "Look, it's late, let's call it a night. We'll get back together with fresh minds in the morning."

"Any reason I can't take the numbers with me?"

"No, go ahead, Chief Payne, but tomorrow Frank's arranged some help from IBM, so don't worry, we'll get it."

"Retired Chief, remember, but lately it sure doesn't seem like it." I looked at Jennings and Winslow. "Ready anytime you are," I paused, "and Mr. Harding, it's what I used to do."

The three-hour time difference was doing a number on me. I rolled to my left, but couldn't get comfortable – the green numbers on the clock-radio showed 1:10. When I last looked they'd glowed 12:55 a.m.

Counting sheep had never been my thing – usually I was out as soon as my head hit the pillow, either too soft or hard like the kind the Holiday Inn seemed to specialize in, it made little difference.

No hurriedly-downed sandwich to blame it on tonight. Groups of 1's and 2's whirled around in my head. I sat up. *What if he's switched back to the Bible? For sure they likely changed the code each day or so, that was standard practice.*

I switched on the light and reached for the nightstand drawer. *Thank God for the Gideon's!*

As if there were someone else in the room, I started talking. "Best bet is that the "P" indicates a book, rather than a page, so let's see. Oh boy, there's two "P" books in the Old Testament, two in the New, that is if you don't include 1st and 2nd Peter."

The Cronus Cypher

Next, assuming the numbers were a combination of either chapter and verse or verse and the letter that began a word, I got a piece of hotel stationery and began. *Just like the old days.* I quietly hummed "Back in the Saddle Again."

An hour later my saddle was well worn, but I'd ridden nowhere. *Time to think like a spy, Herschel.*

Twenty-Five

Somewhere around six-twenty in the morning I couldn't wait any longer and called the number Gerri had given me.

"Good morning, Ramada Inn."

"Room 223, please."

The phone rang, and rang, and after the seventh, the operator came back on. "Sorry sir, no one is answering. Shall I try again?"

"No, I'll call back, oh wait, I'd like to leave a message for Miss Jennings – Herschel Payne called, she has my number."

Now what? Time for a quick shower.

As I started the water, the phone rang. "Hello."

"Hersch, this is Gerri, sorry I wasn't in the room when you called. I was just back from my morning run and the night clerk spotted me and gave me your message. Didn't know you were an early riser. What's up?"

"I'm really not an early riser – didn't sleep … ah, been up most of the night. I think I got it! At least I think I narrowed it down, but now I need some big-time help from NSA's computers."

"Okay, I'll call Spence, take a quick shower and we should be at the Holiday Inn, oh, let's say we'll meet you for breakfast at seven-thirty. Congratulations, you still got the old magic, huh."

I may have the "magic" but I knew I was a long way from the solution, and no bunny rabbit was going to pop out of a hat without some heavy-duty computer assists.

I couldn't believe how hungry I was and when the waitress asked if I wanted to order now or wait for "my friends", I immediately ordered the small stack of pancakes with two eggs over easy, my all-time favorite breakfast.

Halfway through my second cup of coffee, I spotted Winslow and Jennings and waved.

"Good morning. I've already ordered," I said, without apology as they slipped into the booth.

Winslow caught the waitress's eye and she came to our booth and took their orders. "No problem, Hersch, from what Gerri says, you've been up all night."

"Maybe not all, but most of it." I looked around. "Should I tell you what I think here, or …"

"No, let's wait. I did call Harding and told him we'll need some computer time right away. I know you're eager and so are we, but hold on till we get to NSA," Winslow said.

"You have the floor, Herschel," Harding said."

"I made the assumption Cronus switched from The Iliad back to the Bible. Next I took a look at all the books in the Bible that begin with the letter 'P' – there are four, not counting 1st and 2nd Peter. From there I reasoned that the '10' following the 'P' is the chapter in the book. That eliminated Philemon and Philippians that don't have ten chapters, leaving Psalms and Proverbs. I remember Frank said yesterday that Cronus had previously used the Old Testament, so I concluded I was right, Psalms or Proverbs. Okay, now here's what I think. The numbers indicate the verse and word position in the verse. At this point last night I realized I couldn't go any further without computer help – too many combination possibilities. Also, it hit me that there are several versions of the Bible and Cronus could have used any. Here's what I propose. Start with the King James Version, then the New International, then the Revised Standard, and so on, and try all the possible permutations until we get a message that makes sense."

I looked at the six people in the room. Blank stares all around. Winslow cleared his throat.

Harding spoke first. "We've got nothing to lose. Frank, it's time to fire up the IBM 5100 and see if that new software we've got is worth its cost. Gerri, see if you can scrounge up the Bibles we need and, Herschel you and Spencer start roughing out the inputs for Frank and Stan. Okay, let's do it!"

The Cronus Cypher

The Advanced Encryption System, or AES, and the IBM 5100 did the trick, and much sooner than I'd guessed possible Frank, whose last name I'd learned was Stiles, looked up from a printout. "Got it! It's Psalms, Chapter 10, like you guessed Hersch, and he used the NIV. See here, the '17' is verse one, the seventh word – starts with an F; 164 is verse sixteen, word 4, which starts with a K, and so on. Here it is."

The decoded message read: "F K Meet Mon Eight Fifteen."

"Damn," I shouted, "Woody!"

"He's the last one I would have picked," Jennings said.

"Me too," Winslow added. He turned to me. "Sorry, Hersch, but we knew it had to be one of them."

"What now?"

"Good question," he turned to Harding.

"Well, the meeting doesn't start until Tuesday, and President Ford's meeting with President Kekkonen is mostly diplomacy anyway, so that can be any time – the important thing is, our ploy worked and we know the identity of Cronus, but my feeling is we arrest him right away – don't let him participate in the support team for Helsinki."

"Won't his arrest tip off his contact at the embassy?" Winslow asked.

"Maybe … ah, let me think … no, I still think we need to get him out of circulation. Jennings, what's your take?"

"If we can pin down who's the spy at the embassy that would be good, but I'd agree, we can't wait too long. He may already be suspicious and remember, he's a civilian now, and can leave any time he wants. I'd opt to arrest him before the team gets together today."

"What about the agents of theirs in Finland?" I asked. "Aren't they still a danger?"

Twenty-Six

I looked at Woody through the special one-way viewing wall. He was alone in the room and had only been told he was going to be given an additional assignment prior to the start of training session. He didn't appear apprehensive.

I was to observe when the charges were read during the interrogation. A tiny microphone was concealed under the table.

The door opened and Winslow, Jennings and Stan entered, followed by Harding, who took the chair next to Woody. The strategy, I had been told, was to first read him his rights, then immediately confront him with the evidence, pressure for his confession, delaying as much as possible filling any request for an attorney.

"Woody, we've uncovered evidence that seems to indicate you are the mole called Cronus!"

Woody came out of his chair like he had a firecracker up his ass, and I thought for sure he was going to hit Harding, before Winslow and Stan stopped him, but he immediately sat down. "This is a joke, right?"

"No joke." He started to get up again. "Sit down! You have the right to remain silent, anything you say …"

"Kiss my ass, you son-of …"

Agents Stan and Winslow grabbed Woody and forced him down in the chair.

For a moment he said nothing, then looking around, I think to see if I was there, said, "So the whole thing with Hersch about watching Russ, Chief and Mick, that was all a pack of lies?"

"In a way it was. We knew one of you was the mole, but until you fell for our ambush and called your contact at the embassy we didn't know who it was. Herschel Payne was following our instructions – helping to bait the trap, so to speak."

Woody slowly shook his head. "You're wrong, and Hersch, if you're listening, you are a first- class son-of-a-bitch." Then he looked directly at Harding. "Screw Miranda – I am not, nor was I ever a spy for anyone, I am a loyal US citizen, retired Navy and proud of it, and now here's what I want! First, I want to talk to Hersch, and then I want to call someone."

Without looking at the one-way viewing wall, Harding said, "Chief Payne, please join us."

As the adage goes, "if looks can kill, I'd be dead." Woody followed my every move across the floor – his eyes like drill bits boring into me.

Before I could utter a word, he said, "I'd like everyone out of here except Hersch and her," he nodded Gerri's way. "You can watch from wherever you've set up and you can bind my hands to this chair if you want."

Harding and Winslow looked at one another. Harding spoke. "All right. You have all the time you need, and Woody, we will be watching and listening. Hersch, is this okay with you?"

I looked deep into my old friend's eyes – the friend I'd spent so many hours with. "Fine with me, and let's forget any bindings." I glanced at Gerri, and she nodded concurrence.

When the three men had gone, Woody stared at me, then Gerri and then back to me. "All right you two, how in heaven's name did you decide I was the mole?"

Gerri and I exchanged looks and she slowly nodded approval.

I told him how we'd set the trap.

"So as I understand, you pretended to let slip to each of us the time Presidents Ford and Kekkonen would meet at Kekkonen's residence in Helsinki, but each of us were given a different time, in my case eight-fifteen?"

"That's right. You got eight-fifteen; Russ, Chief and Mick each an hour later than the other, starting with nine-fifteen."

"And the message you intercepted and deciphered said eight-fifteen. That's it! I can't …?"

Gerri interrupted Woody. "What other explanation is there? You were the only one given that information and time. Lie as much as you want, Cronus – can I call you Cronus – you are our mole."

Woody hung his head, but I could see a grin on his face. He looked up. "You're dead wrong Hersch. Now I want to call someone and after that I'm done talking."

"Who?" Gerri asked. "You get one call," sounding like a cop in a scene from a B-movie.

"Andy Hetzel. He's not going to believe any of this crap and I'm hoping he can get me an attorney."

Harding and Winslow reentered the room. "One call and we will monitor it. After that, I'll see. Herschel, Jennings, Winslow, anything you'd like to add?"

"No … well there is one question, one thing that has been bugging me all day." I looked at Woody. "You weren't with me at the base in Scotland when our communications team broke the code on the SAM missile's guidance system, so how did the info get to the North Vietnamese so fast? The data was never sent to the other bases for fear the Russians would intercept it and change the signal before we could start jamming again. If you somehow got the info … are you a spy for both North Korea and North Vietnam?"

"For Christ's sake …I don't know what the hell you're talking about, and screw you Hersch. Maybe I don't work for anyone, maybe the Russians. I want to make my call now."

"Stan, get him a phone," Harding said. "Chief Payne, I'll need you to meet with the other three before the training session today, and then take the rest of the day off, get some rest."

Woody didn't look at me as I left the room. Regardless of his guilt, I felt like the world's greatest jerk. Plus something was nagging at me – something I couldn't quite put my finger on – a voice kept saying things just didn't fit. *Scotland,* something about Scotland? *I'm just tired.*

As Winslow watched, Stan connected a phone into the wall outlet and placed it on the conference table next to Woody.

"What's the telephone number? I'll dial it for you." Stan said.

When the connection was made, Stan handed the receiver to Woody.

"Andy, this is Woody. I need your help."

Winslow could only hear Woody's end of the conversation, but he knew the call was being recorded.

"I need a lawyer ... hold on, let me ... ah, I'm being held at NSA, they're accusing me of being some guy named Cronus ... yeah, Cronus – they think I'm a mole for North Korea."

"How? Simple, they laid a little trap for me – listen, just get me a lawyer and I'll ... here, you can talk to this guy named Winslow, yeah, Winslow, he's with NSA. No, ole' Hersch was part of their plan, the asshole, the whole Helsinki thing was a ruse, but ... hold on, I'm not guilty – just call for me, Andy; get me a lawyer, and fast! Here's Winslow."

Twenty-Seven

The meeting with Russ, Chief and Mick hadn't gone well, in fact it went horribly. When I told them of the scam, I thought for sure at least one of them would haul off and smack me. Eventually, they had relaxed and expressed relief that Woody had been caught, even though, like me, they couldn't believe he was guilty of spying. Based on advice from Winslow, I didn't reveal the spy's code name was Cronus. He said we could tell them later when we caught the spy at the Korean Embassy.

Now back in my room at the Holiday Inn, I was stretched out on the bed, trying to fall asleep, but with no success. I turned on the television. A new show, *Wheel of Fortune*, was on one channel, some soap opera on another – too early for the news. I turned it off. *Mark's school paper – perfect.*

I pulled the binder from my suitcase, propped up the bed pillows and began to read my son's paper.

Our family had traveled 4,162 miles in 28 days when we finally drove through the Royal Air Force Base gate at 8:15 p.m. on June 24, 1969. Welcome to Edzell, Scotland.

The Cronus Cypher

My dad found out there would be no base housing for some time, so on advice of my parent's friend Chief Jones, we journeyed to the small community of Laurencekirk and got rooms at the Gardenston Arms Hotel. Laurencekirk was about fifteen miles north of the base towards the city of Aberdeen. It was to be our family of five's home for six weeks.

The hotel was built in the late 1800's and had been used as a stopover for travelers on horseback or horse-drawn vehicles between Aberdeen and Dundee. Our two-bedroom apartment was on the second floor. One of the glaring oddities of our accommodations was my parent's bedroom. It was wallpapered with a spotted leopard skin motif; yellow and black spots everywhere!

Our living quarters were above the local pub and my poor dad never got much sleep before he had to go on the midnight watch, and ...

Somewhere during the reading of Mark's term paper I had dozed off, so when the phone rang, my head jerked back hitting the antique bedstead, and the binder was sent flying.

"Hello?"

"Hersch, this is Andy Hetzel."

"Andy, I know what you're going to say, I'm sorry for ..."

He cut me off. "Listen, you had to do what you were asked to do. Just thought I'd let you know I got a good attorney for Woody and he should be there soon. I still can't believe my ole buddy is a spy, but ... ah, maybe we can get together tomorrow and talk about this some more."

I couldn't see how that could help, and NSA might not want me to talk to anyone about Woody, which is what I figure Andy's aiming at. "Maybe, Andy, I'll have to check with NSA and see what's up, I'm pretty beat right now. I'll give you a call."

"Okay, take care, sorry if I bothered you, just trying to help our old friend."

"No, I'm sorry, just tired. I'll call." I hung up.

I got up and gathered the pages of Mark's term paper. The paper and Andy's call got me reminiscing about Scotland again. Andy Hetzel had been the first one to greet me on the base – a meeting which I remembered started with "Well, well, I'll be damned," and ended with a Doctor Lynch saying, "Well, well, what do we have here?"

A routine physical examination was required of all new men on base and when I was ushered into the exam room, the resident doctor for the Naval Communications Station was busy with another exam, so I was told a corpsman would begin the exam. In walked Andy and after several minutes of catching up he told me to strip, and the doctor would be in shortly.

Andy had stood by while the doctor began, several times chuckling and reminding me that he wouldn't peek.

It was while Dr. Lynch was probing my lower extremities that he uttered his statement "Well, well ..." he'd discovered I had a hernia. And so began my tour of duty in Scotland – a week in the hospital. Mark didn't have that in his paper. *Probably forgot.*

I picked up Mark's term paper and began to read again.

Shortly after we got settled, we met the Drake family and I became good friends with their two boys. Commander Drake was a dentist at Edzell ...

Twenty-Eight

The lobby of the Ramada Inn was a beehive of activity for a weeknight. Formally dressed couples seemed to be moving in every direction at once. Gerri Jennings couldn't imagine the reason for the hubbub until she spied a woman in a flowing white-lace wedding gown emerge from one of the conference rooms, followed by an entourage of couples, men in tuxedos and ladies in powder-blue dresses.

"The pictures are done, everyone can come in now," one of the nattily-attired young men yelled, hoping to be heard over the din.

"Looks like it's a party," Winslow said, surprising Gerri who hadn't heard him come up behind her. "No wonder I couldn't find a parking place until the bottom level."

"It appears we've arrived just in time for the gala wedding reception."

A lady walked by, noticeably weaving and turned back to Gerri. "C'mon, we can go in – I don't know about you, but I'm starved, and they've got an open bar, too."

"I'm starved, too," said Winslow, smiling at Gerri. "It's up to you."

"Hell, why not, I need a change of scenery and who'll even know we're not guests. Should be fun, let's go, but no business talk, okay." With that she took his hand. "We'll be one of the happy couples and from the looks of them; we've got a lot of catching up to do."

They filled their plates and found two empty seats on the outer circle of yet unoccupied tables. The five-piece combo on the stage to the right of the wedding party's table launched into Pink Floyd's new hit single, "Shine On", as Spence rose.

"What do you want from the bar?"

"A glass of Chardonnay, if they have it, please."

Gerri and Spence ate and watched as first the bride and groom, then she and her father, then the groom and his new mother-in-law, and finally the rest of the members of the bridal party paired off for the customary rite of first dances. Two other couples had joined their table and over small talk, Gerri had learned the bride and groom were from Dupont Circle and were going to Bermuda for their honeymoon. When one of the women began asking her some personal questions, Gerri glanced at Spence, pursed her lips and titled her head toward the dance floor.

"They're playing our song, dance my dear?" he said, rising and winking.

"Why thank you kind sir, I'd love to."

With the small difference in their heights Gerri bent to his ear. "By the way, my favorite song is an oldie, *Stardust*, a little slower pace than whatever this is they're playing."

"It's *Love Machine*, by the Miracles."

"Wow, I'm impressed."

"Mine is *Proud Mary*, by the way, and next time we go dancing, wear flats."

She pulled back, looking into his hazel eyes. "Will there be a next time?"

"That's up to you." He pulled her close.

The music ended and they stood apart, her arms still around his neck, his around her waist.

"This is dangerous territory, Spence."

"I know, but ..."

The combo's singer, who didn't come close to sounding like Judy Collins, started singing the pop stars popular *Send in the Clowns*.

"But what?"

"It's dangerous, but damn you feel good," he said, pulling her in once more, but purposely not too close. *Jeez, it's been a while since he's risen to the occasion.* "Probably the wine."

"Yeah, right, it's the wine, even if it is the jug variety. And Spence, you feel good too." She giggled, but didn't pull away.

"Maybe if it gets too noisy and the music's too fast for you, we can adjourn to ... ah, my room, you know ..."

"Now that does sound risky. For the present, I'm just fine dancing with plenty of people around to keep us company."

The Cronus Cypher

Several slow dances and a couple glasses of wine later they stood outside his room. Spence glanced questionably at Gerri, then pulling her close, they softly kissed. She pulled back and looked into his eyes.

"Just as long as we agree it'll be no-strings-attached sex."

"No strings." He said, opening the door.

As soon as the door closed, Spence took her in his arms again, this time kissing her deeply, his tongue probing, hands gently exploring. "Do you …ah need to …"

"Give me a minute."

"Take your time, I've been thinking about this from the first time I saw you, I …"

"Remember, no strings."

A few miles away at the Holiday Inn, Herschel Payne had finished reading his son Mark's term paper.

"I'd forgotten about that," he said aloud.

Something doesn't add up. What was the line Bruce had when he played Marcellus in Hamlet? Hmmm …

"Something is rotten in the state of Denmark!"

The Cronus Cypher

Part Three

The tissue of life to be
    We weave in colors all our own,
And in the field of destiny
    We reap what we have sown.
        – Whittier

The only rose without a thorn
  is friendship *– Anon*

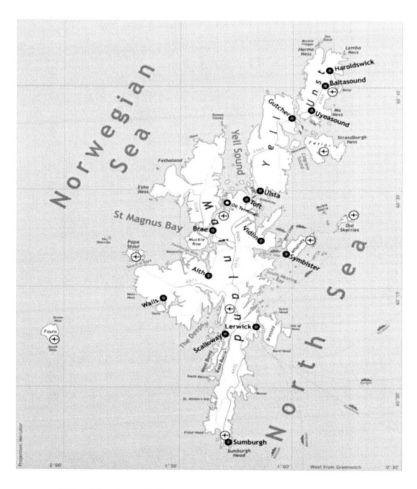

The Shetland Islands (Scotland, United Kingdom)

Twenty-Nine

I waited impatiently as the phone continued to ring. It was half past ten. *Maybe she's still at NSA. No, too late for that.* I hung up and dialed the Ramada's front desk again.

"Can you connect me with Mr. Spencer Winslow's room, please?"

Three rings later there was a groggy-sounding response. "Hello."

"Spence, this is Hersch." *Sounds like I woke him up – damn.*

"Hersch, ah …you're still up, so what … shi … it's going on eleven, can't it wait until tomorrow?"

"No. I think we've overlooked something, and well, Woody may not be our man. I know it's late, but I called Gerri's room and got no answer – I need to take another look at those files if she's got them with her."

He didn't answer at first and I thought it sounded like he was talking to someone in the room.

"I think she does. She's probably downstairs … there was a party going on when we came in, and she said she might check it out … ah, how about we meet you again for breakfast, say about seven. I think we all need a good night's sleep – I know I do. Okay, can it wait?"

I thought to myself, I really didn't want to wait, but guessed I had little choice. "All right, see you both at seven."

I'm not ready to let this go.

This time the phone was answered on the second ring by a familiar voice. "Hello."

"Hi Barb, it's me."

"Hersch. I was hoping it was you. How's it going?"

"Not so good, really. I think I may have helped get a good friend arrested and now I'm not so sure he's guilty, even though we thought the evidence was irrefutable."

"Who's that?"

"Woody Floyd."

"Oh, I can't believe it either – we had such good times with him in the Philippines, and knowing him Hersch, I just don't see him doing anything to hurt our country."

"I know, I feel the same way. Honey, do you recall when I went with Dr. Drake to the Shetlands?"

"The first time?"

"Yes, as I remember it was in March … ah … late March, but I can't remember the exact date, which is important."

"Sorry, Hersch …"

"Is Mark there? I think he may be able to help."

I could hear Barb calling him, and then he was there.

The Cronus Cypher

"Hi Dad, Mom says maybe I can help you."

"I think you might, but first of all, how are you? Are you any closer to your decision on joining up?"

"Yup, think I will for sure, talked to the recruiter again yesterday."

"Great. Mark, I've been reading your term paper. You've really done a fine job, captured all the fun things that happened and I especially like your account of our climb up Mt. Ben Nevis. You describe it so vividly, seems like it was just yesterday."

"Yeah, Mom said she packed it in your stuff."

"Listen, in the first part of your story, you talk about when I went with Dr. Dave to the Shetlands. Do you remember or somewhere in your notes do you have the days I was gone?"

"Hold on."

I waited, hoping that the dates would confirm what I had suspected.

He was back. "You left on a Thursday, March 31st, and returned on the fifth of April."

"How can you be so sure?"

"I wrote it down in my journal – we had a family trip planned to Edinburgh that weekend and had to reschedule it, remember? You were gone five days and I remember too that I got to drive to pick you up at the ferry dock and I was late getting back for a dance that was on the fifth."

"Thank you, Mark, this could really be important. Now, let me say hello to Bruce and Melanie."

Now all I could do was wait until morning. I thought about my three trips to the Shetlands with Commander Dave Drake – great memories, especially the second time ten months later when we were there for "Up-Helly-Aa."

Dave had explained to me that more of the men at the Coast Guard station at the northern sector of the Shetlands needed dental care, and this time he'd scheduled the trip to coincide with the annual end-of-the-holidays festival starting on the last Tuesday of January. On this trip, as before, he needed to have a corpsman along to do the preliminary examinations. I'd jokingly said I could do it, but Dave got Andy Hetzel cleared to go with us again. Andy was all excited because he'd have an opportunity to visit a local tattoo parlor and add a complimentary tattoo to the one he'd gotten on the last trip. On his left shoulder was emblazoned the Imperial German Eagle, now he wanted the Scottish Lion Rampant on the right.

Up-Helly-Aa is a celebration depicting the ousting of the Nordic people that overran the Scottish Isles centuries before. At the height of the celebration the citizens of Lerwick, dressed in period costumes, light torches and burn a symbolic Nordic boat. Of course the gaiety was fueled by many rounds of scotch, and a lime and beer drink called Chandy's, consumed at thirteen halls throughout the community. Somewhere around two a.m., after we'd visited the sixth hall, I decided enough was enough, said goodnight to Andy and Dave, and made my way back to our B & B.

The following year Dave and I returned to the Shetlands and this time we were invited to be a part of the parade group, meandering through town, singing songs and carrying torches.

This time I managed to visit all thirteen halls. I learned later from Dave that we were the first "outsiders" to be invited as a part of the parade group. It was a fond memory and one of my last adventures before my time in the Navy would end.

Thirty

Hae-won had only been asleep a few minutes when the telephone rang.

"Hello," she said tentatively, wondering who would be calling at such a late hour.

"This is Cronus. Do you recognize my voice? I only have a few seconds for this, listen carefully."

"Yes ... but I ..."

"Rhea and Zeus, I repeat, Rhea and Zeus."

The phone went dead.

She'd known this time might come, but was nevertheless panicked by what she'd heard. The code words picked years ago. Rhea the wife of Cronus coupled with Zeus, Cronus and Rhea's son. The meaning – they'd been compromised, found out.

A week earlier Cronus had given her specific instructions on what to do in such a circumstance.

"**D**amn, if that's Hersch again," Spence said rolling away from Gerri and reaching for the phone.

"If it is, take it easy, he's only trying to help."

"Hello."

"Agent Winslow, this is Frank Stiles. Sorry to call you so late, but you did tell me to call at any time if we picked up anything significant on either of the embassy women's home phones."

"No, that's okay. What do you have?"

"The woman named Hae-won just got a call from Cronus."

Spence put his hand over the mouthpiece and turned toward Gerri. "Cronus called the woman named Hae-won, so we know who his contact is for sure now, but … wait awhile."

Hc removed his hand. "He said he was Cronus?"

Frank responded. "Yes, Cronus, hold on, I'll play the tape recording."

Gerri, who by now had risen and retrieved her clothes watched intently as Spence sat on the edge of the bed and listened. "Play it again."

"Have you called Harding yet?" Spence asked when the recording concluded. "If not, call and update him on the latest info. He should probably listen to the taped message, also. I think we should send some agents over to Hae-won's apartment as quickly as possible and pick her up. The message could be a warning for her." He hesitated, listening. "You got me, I thought we had Cronus under lock and key?"

Winslow hung up and turning to Gerri, who was now fully clothed, repeated Cronus' message to Hae-won. "You as confused as I am?"

"For sure. If that's Cronus then either Woody got to a phone, or we've definitely got the wrong man."

"Son-of-a-bitch!" Spence stood up, seemingly unconscious of his nudity. "Guess it's time to come back to reality." He smiled broadly. "By the way, I don't do one-night stands."

"Me neither, but before you go dashing out, I'd suggest you at least pull on your shorts." She chuckled. "You are sorta cute, though."

"Funny."

"I'm going to my room. Let's meet in the lobby in an hour and head in – looks like it's going to be a long night"

"An hour it is, and I'll call Herschel; it sounds like we need to meet with him earlier than expected."

Do we dream in color? I was – reliving our 1973 climb of Mt. Ben Nevis, the spectacular views from the summit, the Glen Coe Valley below, being on top of the world …

At first I imagined the ringing was the dinner bell used by the innkeeper where Mark, Bruce and I stayed during our climbing trip … the phone.

"Hello."

"Hersch," the voice said, "this is Spence, we do need to get together quickly, and before breakfast – something's happened. Can you be ready in … ah, say at two?" He went on to explain about the intercepted message from Cronus to Hae-won.

"So that means Woody is not Cronus."

"Not necessarily, but it sure looks that way," he responded, now sounding less gravelly.

I glanced at the clock-radio. *One-ten.* "Okay, by the way, I think I've got some information that could possibly clarify things for you about Woody."

"That's good. See you around two."

Thirty-One

"Coffee smells good," I said climbing into the back seat and accepting the paper cup from Gerri.

"Spence's idea and we've got donuts, too, courtesy of White Castle."

"Before we get to Fort Meade, I want to tell you what I need."

"All right, Hersch, shoot," Spence answered.

"But I need to give you some background first. It has to do with my time in Scotland." I took a sip of the coffee and started.

"On March 29th, two days before I went to the Shetlands with Commander Dave Drake, our communications section was knee deep in you know what. The North Vietnamese had launched the biggest offensive since Tet, and they caught us with our pants down. We'd had NSA Explorer teams near the Demilitarized Zone since January but when the SAM missile attacks started we couldn't intercept their signals to jam them. We figured either the Russians or North Koreans had gotten wind of our teams and changed signal codes. Finally on March

30th the DMZ team succeeded in intercepting the signal sent by the small spiral antenna of the SAM and transmitted it to our group in Scotland. We deciphered it and they were able to jam it and send their missiles off course. I was set to leave for the Shetlands on the 31st, but couldn't have gone if things changed. By midday on the 31st NSA was still successfully jamming, so I was granted leave to go with Commander Drake.

I found out later that the day we got to the Shetlands, the Russian technicians had received information about our signal acquisition machine, and changed the signal code again. I remember at the time wondering how they'd gotten the information so fast. Of course we eventually were able to jam the signal again, but the damage had been done and many lives were lost."

No one said anything for a minute, I guess waiting for me to go on or say that's it. Spence broke the silence. "So, how does this relate to our spy, who at this point may still be Woody?"

"No one outside of Scotland and the DMZ team knew about any of this at the time. Neither Woody, Russ, Chief nor Mick were ever stationed in Scotland. So my question is, were any of them on the DMZ team, or even better, where was Woody between March 29th and April 4th of 1972?"

We slowed down, showed our badges to the guard and easily found a parking spot in the deserted lot.

"But if it turns out Woody is clear, aren't we right back to square one, and who else knew about our scheme – I mean, only Woody was told eight-fifteen," Gerri said. "There's you, me, Spence, Frank, Stan, and Harding. One of us is Cronus? C'mon get real!"

"Okay, here we are. First thing we do is find out where Woody was on those dates, and maybe even more important, did anyone let him use the phone tonight?"

"As they say, 'the night is young'," Gerri said. "We can start with my file on Woody. Let's go!"

An hour later we'd determined that none of the suspects were with NSA's DMZ team that March and most revealing, Woody was with the communications team in Makalapa, Hawaii at the same time, nor had he phoned anyone after his one call to Andy Hetzel to get an attorney.

Winslow leaned back from the conference room table. "Were we wrong about all of this? I mean, all our evidence points to one of the four being the mole. What we missed is what Hersch has uncovered, that from late March to early April of '72, none of the four were in Vietnam and none of them were ever in Scotland."

"Yet we still have the fact that only Woody was given the eight-fifteen meeting time," Gerri said.

Harding, who hadn't said anything to this point, only grumbling a time or two, pushed his chair back. "Obviously we've overlooked something. Where's Floyd now?"

"At the federal prison over in Cumberland," Frank answered.

"Go get him. Spence, you, Gerri and Herschel need to talk to him as soon as possible – our collective reasoning has definitely gone astray."

"What about his attorney?" Spence asked.

"Get the phone number and invite him or her over here, too. We don't have a lot of time. President Ford leaves for Helsinki in a few days."

Cronus was finally alone again. He'd been through all the scenarios and concluded there was only one person other than Woody Floyd that could put him in harm's way – Herschel Payne.

He thought, *would Hersch remember? It's been a while.*

Cronus had never been in a situation where harming someone physically was required. When indoctrinated years earlier, he agreed to only pass along critical information – that he would take no direct action against anyone. Now he had to consider that possibility. After much deliberation, he'd narrowed down his choices: directly eliminate Herschel Payne; threaten him in some way that would make sure if he did finally put two and two together, he'd keep quiet; or, threaten to harm his family. For the latter choice, he could use Zeus or enlist the help of Ki-woon.

He made his choice.

He'd seldom contacted Ki-woon directly, usually leaving that up to Hae-won, but when he did, he'd used code words only known to Ki-woon, and she in turn would use a preselected response. *Seattle is three hours earlier, so I should catch her at home.*

The phone was answered on the fourth ring. He thought it was her voice.

"The stone is swallowed up."

No response, then the prearranged response, "And Zeus is safe."

"This is Cronus, listen carefully."

Thirty-Two

The Little Patuxent River begins in Laurel, Maryland, passes through some of the most densely populated areas of the state and ultimately merges with the Chesapeake Bay at Solomon's.

"Beautiful, isn't it," Gerri said, as she joined me on the bench at the end of the path. "I forget how peaceful DC can be at dawn, especially when the sun reflects off the water and the only sounds are from the loons on the river."

"Yeah, the Patuxent reminds me a little of the Satsop, except back home fishermen would be lining the banks at this time of the day. Wish I was there, but this is a close second," I said.

"They should be here soon, Hersch, time to get back in."

"I know." I turned to face her. "As they say, 'the calm before the storm'?"

"Looks like it."

"Okay, I guess I'm ready."

The Cronus Cypher

Some three thousand miles away the telephone rang at the Payne residence in Montesano.

Barbara at first thought it was the alarm on the clock-radio. *It can't be seven yet.*

It's the phone! As she reached for the receiver, she glanced at the clock-radio. *Ten after two – good God.*

"Hello?"

No answer.

"Hello?" Barbara hung up.

Five minutes later it rang again.

"Hello – who is this?"

Silence, then a dial tone.

Mark knocked on the bedroom door. "Mom, who's calling at this time of the night?"

"I don't know. Must be a prank – go back to bed."

The phone rang a third time and she was tempted to let it ring, but didn't.

"Hello, if this is a joke …"

"I have a message for you from Cronus," said the voice with a pronounced accent.

"Cronus … ah, who is this?"

"Be quiet and listen. Tell Herschel Payne that we are watching you. We will harm you and your family unless he stops helping the NSA immediately."

Barbara started to say something and the caller hung up. The accent had been definitely oriental, maybe Chinese.

Mark knocked on the door again. "Mom, is everything alright?"

The Cronus Cypher

Woody Floyd was seated in the same chair where he'd been questioned earlier. Across from him sat a man who appeared to be in his early thirties, unshaven and disheveled. The man rose when Spence, Gerri and I entered the room.

"Do you know what time it is, I don't …"

"Please sit down, Mister … ah?" Spence said.

"Cook, Henry Cook, Mr. Floyd's attorney," he answered, sounding very indignant.

During the verbal interchange, Woody kept his eyes down, but when I walked over and sat next to him, he looked me straight in the eyes and seemed surprised that I smiled at him.

"What are you smiling about asshole?"

I looked at Winslow, who nodded, and then I turned back to Woody. "I'm smiling because it looks like we were dead wrong about you. I did feel, as you put, like an 'asshole' and still do, for putting you through this."

"What … you mean …"

Mr. Cook, as they say, 'blew a gasket.'

"Relax, Cook. You heard right, we now believe Mr. Floyd is not the mole. All charges will be dropped, but we still need some answers before we can officially let your client go," Winslow said. "Hersch, you've got the floor …"

"Hold on." Harding walked into the room. "There's an emergency call for Herschel from his wife. I talked to her briefly, but Hersch," he said looking directly at me with a serious expression, "you need to hear this directly from her. C'mon, you can take the call in room 3-C. Spence, you come along, too. Gerri, stay here and get these fellows some coffee – it should be about ten minutes."

163

The Cronus Cypher

I rose and followed Harding. "I don't understand, has something happened at home – someone hurt?"

"Your family is fine," he said opening the door to room 3-C where I saw Agent Frank Stiles was holding a phone receiver.

"Go ahead and talk to your wife Hersch. Spence will listen in on the extension – you'll understand why."

I took the receiver from Frank. "Barb, what is it?"

In a calm voice that flew in the face of the circumstances, Barb told me of the threatening telephone call.

"The voice sounded oriental?" I asked. She replied yes, and said that it reminded her of the Chinese lady at the drycleaners in Elma.

"I think she's Korean," I said.

"Mrs. Payne, this is agent Winslow, I'm on the extension. Listen, we've already called our people in Seattle and they're on the way to your home. The three agents coming are named Les Holcomb, Don Smithers, and Larry Burrows. They'll have ID's to show you …"

I interrupted Spence. "Barb, I'm sorry about this. Put Mark on please."

He must have been standing next to her. "Dad?"

"Mark, listen carefully. Do you remember the German pistol I bought in Scotland – the Luger? Well, I want you to get it out of my closet. Your mom knows where the key is to the box and ammunition, I'll hang on."

At the moment the strange tale of the 9mm Luger seemed almost surreal. It had been on our last trip to Edinburgh when I spotted the pistol in a gun shop and couldn't resist buying it. And what a history the pistol had …

Mark was back on the phone. "I've got it, Dad."

"All right. You've fired the weapon before at the firing range near Lake Sylvia, so I want you to load it and keep it handy. If anyone attempts to break in before the NSA men get there, you protect our family. I'm counting on you, son, now put your mom back on."

Winslow nodded, while I talked to Barb, and then Bruce and Melanie.

When I hung up he said, "Do you think that's a good idea? I mean having him there with a gun."

"He's nineteen and quite capable, unless you've got a better idea. Hell, whoever called may be in town already. I can't take a chance."

"But how will they know whether you continue to help us or not?" Spence asked.

"They seem to know everything else!" I offered. "And I am going to continue."

"Okay," Spence said. "Curious – how'd you end up with a German Luger?"

As we walked back to room 3-B I gave him a quick summary of the saga of the Luger.

I'd learned from the shop owner that a lady brought the pistol to the gun shop because it was against the law for her to have firearms in her home. Her husband, who had recently died, had gotten it off a dead German Officer, and against the law, had concealed it when he returned to England in '45. Ultimately, he'd buried it in his backyard and every so often would dig it up so he could retell the story of how he'd found it.

The Cronus Cypher

I had to leave it in the gun shop to comply with their laws, so when I got discharged I arranged to have the shop owner mail me the pistol, but eventually I received a letter from our government stating they'd determined the Luger was a war artifact and could not be shipped into the U.S.

"What … then how …" Spence said, as we started to enter the room.

"That's the real interesting part of the story," I said, as we paused and I continued telling him the saga of the Lugar.

Earlier this year the Olympia Highland Pipe and Drum Band took a goodwill trip to Scotland. Our local vet, Doc McDonald was a member of the band. So I asked Doc if he could do me a favor when they visited Edinburgh, after explaining my problem. When he returned he called and said he had a present for me. How had he done it? He had the shop owner dismantle the Luger and they placed the pieces in and around the bagpipes that he had purchased. I got a package of parts, but thanks to German efficiency and a manual showing the dismantled arrangement, I resurrected the pistol to its original state.

"As Paul Harvey says, 'and that's the rest of the story'."

"Quite a story too, Hersch." He reached for the doorknob. "It's time to see what we can find out from Woody that will shed some light on this holy mess."

Thirty-Three

The atmosphere in room 3-B was not exactly like walking into a birthday party, but it was virtually the same, because in a sense it was a birthday, one celebrating a rebirth for Woody.

"I got you guys some coffee too, but it's probably cold by now," Gerri said. "What's the deal?"

Harding took the lead on that one. "Well, Gerri, here it is in a nutshell. The 'deal' as you put it is someone, the mole or one of his cohorts, has threatened Herschel's family. They seem to be convinced that Hersch knows something that will reveal facts, which at this point to us are esoteric to say the least."

Woody spoke for the first time. "Esoteric, you say. Pretty big word for this early in the morning, but I gather you chaps are finally convinced I'm not the mole. Gerri here certainly thinks so – another black guy freed from bondage. Sorry if I sound a bit pissed, but who wouldn't be."

"You've got a right to be mad," I said, sitting down next to him. "But here's the thing. Even though I'm convinced, especially when I flashed back to what happened in Scotland, I'm sure Spence and Gerri and the rest still can't reconcile the fact we told no one else the supposed eight-fifteen meeting time for Ford and Kekkonen."

"Yes," said Spence, how can you explain that?"

Woody shook his head. "I can't."

"How about we go over your timetable after you left Fort Meade," Gerri said.

She turned to the attorney. "Mr. Cook, you don't have to stay for this. In fact, what we're going to get into is classified. If there's any charge for your services, send the bill to me at this address." She handed him her card. "Frank will walk you to your car."

Cook shook hands with Woody. "If I can ever help you again, give me a call. Andy said he couldn't believe you were guilty, and he was right. Take care and," he turned to Spence and I, "hope you catch the bad guys."

As soon as Frank and the lawyer left, Gerri turned back to Woody. "Okay, let's start with right after your meeting with Hersch."

Slowly, and with occasional questions interjected by all of us, Woody recapped from the time he left me until he arrived back at one o'clock the next day for the briefing.

Spence spoke first. "So you drove to your house, changed clothes and then met Andy Hetzel at the Bombay Club at seven."

"Yes, it was a little after 1900 hours, or if you prefer, seven p.m."

"How long were you there?" Spence asked.

"Maybe till eleven, eleven-thirty, not any later, I was tired and we'd had one too many beers."

"After you left Andy, you went straight home and then the next morning you went nowhere until you left for Fort Meade, is that right?"

"That's what I said," he glared at Harding.

"And you talked to no one over the telephone?" Harding added.

I'd said nothing at this point, but a thought kept churning around in my brain, trying to get out – a thought that once again led me back to Scotland.

In a voice loud enough that everyone turned to look at me, I said, "Did you tell Andy?"

Woody jerked. "I …no …ah, I don't think … ah, we did talk about you and our times together, and, I don't know, we had quite a few beers …"

"So you can't be sure?" I continued, looking at him directly.

"No …but, even if I did let something slip, and I'm not say'n I did, Andy's true-blue, always has been, jeez, he's been there for all of us."

"Woody, we'd like you to stick around – give us a hand in sorting out this mess," Harding said. "If you agree, we'll keep this between those of us in this room." He looked at Spence, Gerri, then at me. "That alright with you three?"

We all said yes.

"Great, now here's what I suggest. With Frank and Stan's help, you gather every piece of info on Hetzel you can, analyze it, and let's meet back here in, say two hours. In the meantime, I'll have some agents shadow Hetzel, watch his house and be ready to grab him if we conclude he may be our man. Questions? – if not, let's get at it."

The Cronus Cypher

An hour later, Spence, Woody, Frank, Stan and I listened as Gerri summarized the results of our combined inputs.

"Andy Hetzel was born in Philadelphia in 1933 to Fredrick and Mary Hetzel. The Hetzels were married in Germany in 1931 and immigrated to the United States in 1932." Gerri hesitated, "Now get this that Frank dug up. When they entered the U.S.A. at Ellis Island, Mrs. Hetzel's given name was not Mary, it was Kim. Frank dug deeper and could only determine that Andy's mother's parents were Korean and, Hersch clearly remembers Andy telling him his grandparents, the mother's folks were killed in 1952 in a bombing raid at Pyongyang – that's in North Korea, by the way. Now the rest of this, we know from his service record. Andy went to Radioman School, but didn't make it through Communication Technician School. After he failed CT School, he successfully qualified for what the Navy calls A-School for medical corpsmen and took classes at Great Lakes, Illinois. After that he took training to become a Hospital Corpsman and later qualified for advanced training so he could serve both ashore and at sea. During the past twenty-one years Hetzel has served in – get this, Japan, Guam, Hawaii, on board three vessels including the *Yorktown*, two assignments here in Maryland with NSA, and as Hersch has reminded us, in Scotland. Currently he's at Bethesda. So, had we put him in the mix when we were matching up CT people to the times the mole sent crucial information, Hetzel would have been at the top of the list! Especially when you factor in the SAM missile intercept mission in '72."

I was the first to speak. "But, how did Andy learn of all the secret information. I mean, he wasn't directly involved – no, it just doesn't make sense ... and yet it does. Now what?"

"Let me give Harding a call," Spence said, "see what he thinks."

Thirty-Four

I've been a hunter, but never the hunted, so as we waited for Jacob Harding I wondered if Andy had any idea he was potentially to be our prey but at the same time, I realized if Andy was the mole, he had already put my family in the same position – they could be the hunted.

I was raised in a family of hunters. The success of the hunt meant meat for the winter and each family member was expected to bring home at least one deer or elk. In 1951, I'd waited all season to go on a hunting trip; but there never seemed to be room for a sixteen year old, however my dad made sure I was included on the last day of the season when we would hunt along the West Branch of the Satsop River.

Dad let me use his single shot 12-guage shotgun and when everyone went their separate directions, or "fanned out" as my uncle had said, I got up on a log and placed a buckshot shell into the rifle's chamber – and waited, and waited. After what seemed like hours I heard a clump-clump-clump sound – the sound of hooves hitting the ground. No human could move that fast, so when I saw the ferns move about 300 feet away, I fired.

I quickly jumped down from the log and looked behind the ferns. On the ground lay a spike buck deer.

Later that day I spotted another deer trying to climb up a bank by the river coming toward me. I cocked the shotgun, brought it to my shoulder in one smooth motion and fired. My second deer of the day, and as it turned out I was the only one of the hunters to even get a shot off.

The second deer was a female and realizing she could have borne kids the next year, I began to feel less proud of myself for killing a beautiful and helpless animal – that, coupled with the horrific smell of protruding entrails led me to a decision to never hunt again.

When we returned, my grandmother had smiled and said, "It looks like we now have another grownup in the family."

I didn't say much, as I recall, but I do remember her comment had made me feel proud once again, but I still resolved to end my days as a hunter. So here I am today, twenty-four years later where ironically I'm potentially both hunter and hunted.

Spence found me sitting in one of the lobby chairs. "Hersch, Harding's here, c'mon."

"What's he think?" I asked as we walked to room 3-B.

"He says it looks like we've got our man, and to bring him in now, but Gerri and I think we should keep him under watch, don't let him escape and wait to grab him after we've got both the embassy spies – don't want to tip them off."

"We know who the spy is at the Washington D.C. embassy, but still don't know who it is at the legation in Seattle. He or she is probably the person who called my house."

"You're right, and we're hoping if we can quickly arrest this woman Hae-won, she'll give up the Seattle contact."

"Okay, but some thing's still don't add up. As I said before, Andy couldn't have gotten all the info on his own, unless he had direct access to the communiqués."

"He got the meeting time from Woody, didn't he? Maybe that's what he did all the other times, got you guys drunk or maybe you unintentionally let something slip." He opened the door to 3-B. "Here we are, we'll see what Harding's got for us."

You could have cut the tension in the room with a knife.

"Sit down Hersch, Spence. As they say, 'we've got some good news and some bad news.' The good is we're fairly sure Andy Hetzel is still at his home; the bad is, and it's really bad, the two agents assigned to pick up Hae-won came up empty-handed. She's gone. Not at the embassy and not at her apartment."

He continued, "Unless you see any reason now why we shouldn't, Spence, I think we should pick up Hetzel."

"No, I agree," Spence said, "Let's get him, I'll call the team that is watching his house. Any word yet from our guys in Seattle?"

"Not yet, but they should be at Hersch's place shortly." Harding looked at his watch. "Hersch, you and Woody should stay here for now, and as far as Callgrove, Collins and O'Brien are concerned, let's keep them out of the loop, until this is all sorted out."

"What about their part in our team for the Helsinki operation?" Spence asked Harding.

"Go ahead on that as planned. I can't see any reason not to."

Thirty-Five

The seeds of hate Andy Hetzel held for the government of the United States had been planted in 1952 and diligently cultivated by his mother. Every year thereafter she tended her crop, judiciously adding the fertilizers of vengeance. His wife Ruth, however, had no knowledge of Andy's duplicity or of the damage he'd done to US intelligence and the harm to the citizens of the country she loved.

When Ruth Hetzel heard the door chime ring she figured it must be Andy, as she'd found his keys on the hall table and guessed he'd forgotten them when he went for a run earlier. Andy often took a run before leaving for the night shift at Bethesda, but he was usually back by this time.

He'd been unusually affectionate before leaving, uncharacteristically melancholy, but she'd chalked it up to his demanding schedule at the hospital – lately they hadn't gotten a chance to spend much time together. Ruth had also thought it was strange when he'd gone through the garage to take the path that led to the alley, instead of using the front door…

"Just a second," Ruth called as she walked from the kitchen. "You're going to be late."

Odd, it's not locked, she thought as she opened the door.

"Andy …

Andy had seen the men watching his house several hours earlier, and he figured it was only a matter of time. Years ago he'd prepared and hidden in the garage what he jokingly called his escape hatch – a change of clothes and a small case containing what he needed to escape and assume a new identity.

From his vantage point a block away, he saw two men go to the rear of the house; two station themselves on each side, and two more walk up the stairs and push the doorbell.

Cronus turned away from the hedge and walked to the bus stop.

He surmised Herschel Payne either hadn't gotten the warning message or had ignored it, but it seemed obvious his cover had been blown. *I wonder if Zeus knows? He'd better not assume he's off the hook! I'll give him a call.*

Here comes the bus – sorry Ruth, and good luck searching the garage fellows.

"**O**h, I thought it was my husband, I … what? …"

"Mrs. Hetzel, agents Dave Brown and Bill Dexter," the taller of the two said, showing her his NSA identification. "We need to talk to your husband."

"He's not back yet from his run. What's this about?"

"It's a matter of national security, ah … when did Andy leave?"

"About an hour ago, he's usually back by now."

"Mrs. Hetzel, I'm sorry, but we need to search the house." He handed her an envelope. "You'll find our search warrant in this."

Agent Brown didn't wait for a response. "Bill, you take the garage, I'll bring Winslow up-to-date and then start upstairs. Be careful, Hetzel may have come back."

Winslow grabbed the phone's receiver on the third ring. "You're kidding – damn! How'd he get away? Okay, okay, I'm not pointing a finger at anyone. What? – Yeah, search the house and bring his wife – Jesus, what the hell was that …"

Spence jerked the phone away from his ear.

"Dave, you still there, Dave?" he said, continuing to listen.

Spence turned to me. "Shit, half the house is gone – Bill and the others… Dave, hold on …"

"What is it?" I asked.

"The bastard must have booby-trapped the house … what?" Spence was listening again. "The garage? How many? You okay … his wife …

I listened as Spence continued talking to Dave. The gist of what happened was that before he ran, Andy had apparently armed an explosive device in the garage and it had blown when Agent Bill had entered. Bill and one other agent were in critical condition, another was seriously injured. Dave and Ruth Hetzel had a few scratches, but were otherwise okay. Andy was long gone.

Thirty-Six

The three Chief Petty Officers sat at a table in the cafeteria finishing their lunch and killing time until they were to report for duty as part of the Helsinki support team.

He removed the vibrating pager from his pocket and noted the number. "Looks like I've got a call. Be right back," said the Master Chief who had been given the code name Zeus.

They'd gotten the pagers in April and this was only the third time he'd received a page to call Andy.

He took the stairs to the lobby where he'd earlier seen two pay phones. Neither was in use.

The phone was answered on the first ring. "Yes. I don't have a lot of time, so pay attention."

The Master Chief knew by his control's voice tone that all was not well. *Am I in danger?* He listened as Andy Hetzel, code name Cronus, talked.

"They were at my house. I've been compromised, but they'll pay for it. The only thing I can guess is they somehow figured Woody was not their man and linked him to me. They cleverly used the times of Ford's meeting as a ploy, so when I called and gave the time as eight-fifteen ...?

He interrupted Andy. "What! When I told you I had the meeting time, you said you'd already gotten it from Woody – you never asked me what the time was, you idiot ..."

"I know that now! Shut up, so I goofed – at least they don't know about you," Andy said.

"They haven't said anything about Woody or you to us. Are the NSA guys going to find anything at your place that leads them to me?"

"Don't you worry your sweet candy ass about it. Here's what I want you to do."

"What took you so long?" his two buddies asked.

"I had a lot of catching up to do. So, we might as well head to the ops room and get started, c'mon."

The three friends walked down the hallway to the operations room.

"What about the Piping Over Ceremony you asked us to go to at five today, Mick?" Russ asked.

"We should have plenty of time to get there. I'm going to ask Hersch to go also. It's too bad about Woody, he'd have enjoyed it too."

"Yeah, I still can't believe it."

"Look, there he is now," Chief said, spotting Hersch with Gerri outside the entrance.

"So, we tell them nothing about Woody or what happened at Andy's?"

Gerri shook her head. "No, we may have to soon, but for now, Harding wants them kept out of the loop."

I didn't agree, but said okay and turned to greet my friends. "Russ, Chief, Mick, you're right on time. Unfortunately, the last training session has been postponed until tomorrow."

"But doesn't the op start tomorrow?" Russ asked.

Gerri answered. "It does, but we'll start early in the morning and with the time difference between here and Finland, there will be plenty of time to be ready. Sorry for the mix-up."

"That's okay, I was worried we wouldn't have time to get to the Piping Over ceremony at five – now we will," Mick said.

"Piping Over ceremony?" I asked.

"Yup, and you're invited," said Mick. He looked at Gerri uncertainly.

"No reason you can't go, Hersch. Spence wants to talk to you for a while, but there should be time."

"Great," said Mick. "We'll pick you up at your hotel at four."

Ki-Woon cautiously answered the phone on the fifth ring. *It can't be Cronus*, she thought. "Hello."

"You're supposed to wait until I call again and then answer on the third ring," Zeus said.

"I …

"Never mind – this is Zeus delivering a message from Cronus. You are to do two things. First, continue to call Herschel Payne's home. Second, and this is most important, get a message to your contacts in Helsinki and give them the following information: 'Time of Ford and Kekkonen meeting is wrong, repeat the time was not correct. Await further instructions'."

Ki-woon started to ask about Cronus, but all she heard was a dial tone.

The meeting with Spence and Harding had not left me in a good mood. In fairness they were looking out for my own good, but telling me to pack and be ready to leave at eight tonight for home rubbed me the wrong way. Their argument was I should be with my family and they could handle things here. Andy was on the run and they were convinced they would arrest Hae-won soon. When I brought up the situation of the North Korean spy in Seattle, they said that was even more reason for me to get back, although they believed an arrest would be made soon.

Harding said I should enjoy the afternoon with my friends and thanked me again for my help. An NSA agent in Seattle would meet me at the airport and drive me to Montesano.

Thirty-Seven

I recall being notified that my release date from the Navy would be 23 October 1973. In the first part of September, the personnel office informed me I was to be officially "piped ashore" in recognition of my upcoming discharge. "Piping Over" is a longstanding tradition in the Navy when a serviceman retires.

The day of the ceremony and our last day at the Edzell base, Captain Martin presented a Certificate of Appreciation to Barbara for her dedication as a Navy wife and then he told her and the kids to leave the building first. At that point I was a little apprehensive of what to do next.

As I exited the administration door, I became aware of many Chiefs lined up on both sides of the walkway and then I heard the piping whistle sound it's shrill signal. As I saluted the flag, I asked the Chief in charge, "Permission to go ashore". He replied, "Permission granted." Then all the Chiefs came to attention and saluted as I walked down the pathway. Barb and the children watched from a distance as I received the honor from my fellow comrades. Quite a ceremony and to this day, the memories cause me to get a lump in my throat.

The ceremony today was for a close friend of Mick's and it seemed like old times. I would have enjoyed participating; however, ever present was the apprehension of what lay ahead and besides, not being in uniform precluded my direct involvement.

The chief in charge this day blew the piping whistle, all the Chiefs saluted, and then it was over.

"What time's your flight?" Chief Callgrove asked as we walked back to the car.

"Eight, but I need to check out."

"Time for some dinner, you know we may not see each other for a while?"

"Sure, how about Russ and Mick?"

"Russ can go, but Mick wants to stick around here for a while and party with his friend."

The drive to the Dulles International Airport with Spence and Gerri seemed surreal. Only a few days earlier I'd not known either of the NSA agents and now, after working closely with them for days in Washington D.C., I was leaving behind all the intrigue we'd shared together and returning to my life of a retired Chief Petty Officer in peaceful, rural Montesano, Washington. At least I hoped it would be peaceful. Spence had received a message that the Seattle NSA men had arrived at my home and nothing eventful had happened, but because Barbara had received two more anonymous threatening phone calls, the agents were on high alert.

Spence and Gerri had asked about my afternoon with Chief, Russ and Mick and I'd told them all about the "Piping Over" ceremony and very enjoyable dinner with Russ and Chief. For my own part during the drive, I'd noticed a change in the way Gerri and Spence interacted – subtle, but obvious to me anyway. There was a softer, gentler tone to their conversation with each other.

Spence took the off-ramp to the passenger boarding area and stopped at the United Airlines sign.

"Here we are. Got your tickets, don't you?" Spence said, turning towards me. "You don't have a lot of time."

"I have," I laughed. "But, it won't seem quite the same sitting in tourist after coming out in a Lear jet. You know, I'll actually miss you two. Hope you catch Andy and … take care."

"You too, Hersch. Oh, and we've got a little surprise for you when you get on the plane," Gerri said.

"You got me a first class seat?"

"Wait and see – it's a nice surprise. Have a safe trip and call me when you get home." said Spence. We shook hands and when I offered my hand to Gerri, she reached out and pulled me in for a quick hug.

"Seat 17A, you're on the right," the attractive stewardess said checking my boarding pass.

"Thanks …I …" *son-of a gun, it can't be!* But it was.

"Howdy, partner."

"Woody."

"Yup, in the flesh – Winslow and Jennings thought you needed some company and I needed to get away. Who knows, maybe I'll end up helping catch the bad guys, at least I can help you protect your family if those bastards try anything, and besides it'll be good to see Barb and the kids again."

I swung into the aisle seat. "Damn, it's good to see you."

"Me too, you old shellback!"

"I'm sorry Woody about …"

"You're forgiven, c'mon relax – this is a non-smoking section, by the way. It'll be good for us."

Thirty-Eight

Spence eased up on the gas pedal of his '72 Pontiac and glanced out the window. "How much farther?"

"Just three blocks. It's a gray, two-story. It'll be on the right side," Gerri said.

Their conversation since dropping Herschel Payne off at the airport had been exclusively about business: the improved condition of the injured agents, how they'd catch the mole Andy Hetzel, find and arrest the Korean Hae-won, and their mutual success at convincing Harding to let Woody fly west with Herschel.

"I would have given a bundle to see Hersch's expression when he got on that plane and saw Woody," Spence said, pulling his car into the curb. "Nice neighborhood."

"Thanks, ah … damn, I wasn't going to take this any further … I – you want to come in for a while?"

Spence smiled, turned off the ignition and released his seat belt. "I thought you'd never ask."

"Is that right?"

Gerri opened the door, stepped aside and with a hand flourish, motioned for Spence to enter. "I don't have any red wine, I ..."

He turned suddenly and pulled her against him. "That can wait."

Either the unexpected contact with his chest, or the shock of his swift move, left her speechless, transfixed. She found her voice. "Spence ..."

"Shh." His hazel eyes held her mesmerized as he pushed slightly away, reached behind under her sweater and unhooked her bra. Even then she didn't move. Not until he began to gently caress her breasts did she even breathe. She felt like every cell in her body was on high alert, ready to go into action.

"That maneuver is not in the NSA training manual," she uttered eagerly.

"No? Hmm, thought I read it somewhere in there."

"Oh, you learned well, probably lots of homework."

"I'm out of practice, though."

"Doesn't feel like it ... oh ..."

Spence again sought her lips, then nibbled her ear. "Where's your bedroom?" he whispered.

"Down the hall, there – this is really ... remember, no commitment ..."

He picked her up and carried her into the room. They fell onto the bed where their mutual caressing was filled with a heightened passion neither had experienced. Clothes were quickly removed and with them the discarded thoughts of the day's intrigues and drama.

We'd talked during take-off, ascent, and for a few minutes after the Boeing 727 reached cruising altitude, and then both nodded off and slept soundly until the stewardess tapped me to offer peanuts and something to drink. I said "sure" and looked at Woody in the window seat. He was still out cold, but when she popped the tab on the 7-Up can he stirred, grumbled something I couldn't understand – probably lucky for it, and sat up.

"I'll have a beer," he said, "Bud, if you've got it."

She pulled out a drawer in her cart and opened a can of Budweiser. "That'll be two dollars, sir."

"Jeez," he said, I can remember when a beer only cost you six bits."

"Me too, especially in Japan when you could get a big bottle of Kirin for less than that."

"That was Chief's favorite as I remember," Woody said.

"Yup. Speaking of Chief, I wonder how he and Russ and Mick are doing?"

The stewardess reached across me and handed Woody his beer. "Did you say something about Kirin beer?" she asked, taking Woody's five-dollar bill.

"Yes," I said, "we used to get it in Japan when we were stationed there. Why?"

"Oh, I just thought it odd that it's the second time today someone's asked about Kirin beer."

"Someone on this flight?" asked Woody.

"No, a man in the lounge at Dulles Airport where I had dinner, asked the bartender about Kirin. Oh, here's your change, we'll be starting our descent into Chicago in a half hour."

Woody took a big swig of his beer. "How long do we have between flights at O'Hare?"

Andy Hetzel looked across the aisle out the left window at snowcapped Mount Rainier as the plane banked right, then left and started its slow descent over Elliot Bay. Off to the right, the sun was setting over The Brothers in the Olympic Mountain Range. If all went according to plans, Ki-woon would pick him up outside baggage claim. Hopefully, the change to light brown hair, the added horned-rimmed glasses and mustache wouldn't freak her out when he opened the door to her car.

In two days, they would drive to Canada and fly to Seoul. That left him plenty of time for some major payback if Ki-woon had followed his instructions. Andy had laughed to himself about his little pun – he was going to leave the Payne's in *pain.*

He recognized Ki-Woon's car as she drove up to the entrance outside the Northwest Airlines baggage claim area, and walked to the driver's side door.

Ki-woon was momentarily taken aback, but then rolled down the window as the person she didn't initially recognize, greeted her.

"Annyeong, Uhm-ma."

Thirty-Nine

The lights of downtown Seattle came into view as the plane descended lower and lower over the waters of Puget Sound. It was certainly unlike landing in a DC-3, where the windows are not placed for passenger visibility. I remembered my landing on Johnson Island in 1955. I could see only a portion of the island as we had circled for a landing and to this day I swear we were going to plop in the ocean just before I heard the tires hit the runway.

"What ya think'n about?" Woody asked, as I pulled away from the window and checked my seatbelt.

"Oh, that time in '55 when I flew to Guam from Hawaii and we stopped at Johnson Island. I never thought that old DC-3 was going to make the runway."

Woody continued looking out his window. "Too dark down there now, but I bet no palm trees are around here."

"Thank goodness for that. I'll trade the fir trees and cooler weather anytime over a few coconut palms and the heat and humidity. I remember how I sweated in my dress blue uniform for four hours before we refueled and took off. No thanks, the good old Northwest beats 'm all."

The *fasten seatbelt* sign illuminated, and the stewardess reminded us to "return our seats to the upright position".

"Here we go," Woody said. "I hope your townsfolk won't be too shocked to see a colored man like me walking their streets."

"C'mon, Woody," I joked, "I think we must have at least one other black guy in Montesano, maybe even two."

After he introduced himself and had shown us his ID, Agent Larry Burrows helped load our bags into the trunk of his Chevrolet. During the three hour drive to Montesano, Burrows told us since their arrival at my home they'd spotted no suspicious-looking people in my neighborhood, though there had been two more threatening calls. Two agents were currently watching the house. I knew most of this, other than the most recent threat, because I'd called Barb from Chicago. However reassured I was by his assessment, the sooner we got home, the better.

"Where are you staying in Montesano?" I asked, as we reached the outskirts of West Olympia and took the turnoff to Highway 8.

"We're at the Plum Tree Motel. Winslow got a room for Mr. Floyd there, too."

"Oh," I said, "I think we have room at our house for "Mr. Floyd." I smiled at Woody.

He smiled back. "You can call me Woody, young man, but Hersch, maybe for a couple of nights it'll be better if I can stay there. We can see how it goes, okay?"

"Okay, but when Barb knows you're here, she'll probably insist you stay with us."

"Maybe – let's see what's going on for sure, then decide," Woody said, "but I still think at least for tonight you two need some alone time." He chortled and poked me in the ribs.

As we passed the Elma exit and got closer to home, my thoughts drifted back to last year, my first as a civilian. My retirement pay was to be based on my rank and I started receiving fifty-one percent of my pay at the time of separation. We had realized right away it would not be enough to sustain a livable lifestyle. I also knew that with only a high school education, my employment options would be limited, so I had immediately applied for the G. I. Bill and made application to Grays Harbor Community College in Aberdeen. I'd been thirty-eight when I started school – one of the oldest guys at the college. It had bothered me at first, but eventually I thought to myself, "If you can't accept me as I am, stuff it!"

"Here we are," Burrows said, as he slowed and we exited into downtown Montesano.

"Hersch!" Woody said. "You awake?"

"Yup, just reminiscing."

Burrows drove under the Plum Tree's entryway. "Woody, sign in and get your key and then we'll go to the Payne's."

"Okay, but let's get some coffee on the way, it's been a long day."

"I'm sure Barb will have the coffee on, Woody," I said.
"Sure, but I'm hungry too. We can pick up some donuts."

A mile away at the Town Center Motel, Andy Hetzel was looking over the supplies his mother had purchased. After her husband, Andy's dad, had died, she'd started going by her original given name, Ki-woon or Kim for short, as Fred had often called her. She'd never liked the name Mary that the immigration people had written on her papers. The stupid man had said he couldn't pronounce her Korean name, so he was giving her an American name.

"It look's like everything is here. Good job."

"I think this is a bad idea, son."

"I thought you wanted revenge on the people who killed your parents, dropped bombs on them – what do you think I've been doing for all these years."

"But we can leave now and …"

"Be still! Hand me that box of cartridges."

Forty

Spencer Winslow thought he had set his clock-radio alarm to buzz at six a.m. so he panicked when he rolled over and saw the time was seven-ten. *Five hours sleep rather than four*, he thought, *oh well, so I'll be a bit late.* Leaving the warmth of Gerri's bed had been difficult to do and although he'd been severely tempted to stay the night, they'd mutually decided it was not a good idea.

He stared in the bathroom mirror. "You're caught, buddy," he said, "hook, line and sinker!"

The morning's meeting was to start at eight-thirty. "Time to hustle, lover boy."

He set his electric razor down as the phone rang. "Now what?" he said aloud retreating to the bedroom.

"Hello."

He listened as his boss Jacob Harding told him of a new, startling piece of information uncovered by NSA with the help of the FBI – perhaps the final piece of the puzzle. The spy at the Korean legation in Seattle had been positively identified as a woman named Ki-woon Park. After her husband had died the woman legally changed her name, reverting to her original Korean name. Her married name had been Mary Hetzel – Andy's mother. Harding further reported Ki-woon had not shown for work yesterday and when the local agents went to her apartment she was not there. The apartment superintendent told one of our men he had seen Ki-woon getting into her Chevy Monte Carlo around one p.m.

The first question Spence asked when Harding paused was, "Do you think Andy may be heading to Seattle?"

Harding answered, "He may be, or they could be meeting any place, or going their separate ways."

"If we've got a description of her car and a license number maybe we'll get lucky," Spence said.

"Already taken care of, but it's only a little after four on the west coast. Anyway, get in here as fast as you can. You might want to call Jennings and pick her up on the way."

"Maybe we ought to call our guys in Seattle that are watching Hersch and his family."

"Stiles is about to do so, see you soon." And Harding hung up.

Getting used to the three hour time difference had proven to be more difficult than I had imagined, especially when I stayed up past midnight listening to everyone acquaint me with their latest projects following my long overdue and lengthy recounting of my own "project" for the past few days.

The Cronus Cypher

It had been a needed family meeting and no matter what NSA thought, and I really didn't give a hoot, I decided it was time to bring Barb and the children up-to-date. After all, they'd been put into danger because of my volunteering. It was one thing to place them in jeopardy when I was in the Navy and World War III appeared eminent, quite another thing in peacetime.

First I told them about my sessions with Gerri and Spence at the Plum Tree Motel, then the interviews in Washington D.C., where we'd set a trap for the mole, then the breaking of Cronus' cypher, and finally, the subsequent arrest of Woody Floyd.

Without too much of the nuts and bolts details, I explained how we'd ultimately broken the code on the message sent by Cronus … Mark had interrupted at that point.

"So because the message said eight-fifteen and that's what you'd told Woody you concluded he was the mole?" he'd asked.

"Yes, son, and only when I realized because of the dates of the DMZ project in Vietnam, Woody couldn't have known about the frequencies, did we start to suspect Andy Hetzel. By the way, Mark, without your school report on Scotland, I'd have never put two and two together." I'd said, and continued.

I told them about the raid on Andy's house and how lucky the NSA agents had been to escape without serious injury and then how on my last day in DC I had gone to the piping over ceremony with Mick, Russ and Chief. It had brought back poignant memories of my own ceremony. Finally I related the enjoyable surprise when I found Woody on my flight to Seattle. This time it was Bruce that spoke up.

"So Andy is the mole and he's on the loose?"

"Yes, Bruce," I'd said, "and that's why the NSA agents are watching our house – he could be here in Montesano. Someone called and threatened your mom, not him, but somebody who could be just as dangerous …."

Barb had interrupted at that juncture and suggested maybe it was getting late. I realized I might be giving the kids more information than they needed, so I nodded at her and concluded by saying I was home now and I was sure everything was going to be fine.

Even though it was late, the children insisted it was their turn to bring me up to date.

Melanie was excited to tell about her Highland dancing lessons and the recital that was coming up in a week. Bruce was to have a starring role in a play, "The Boy Friend" and was trying out for the role of Petruchio in the Grays Harbor Production of "The Taming of the Shrew."

Mark said he would join the Navy next month, entering into "The Delayed Entry Program" which would put a six-month hold on his entry and allow him to finish his coursework at Grays Harbor Community College in Aberdeen. Barb had exiting news too. She had been accepted to be a graduate assistant at a forthcoming Dale Carnegie Course.

Now, looking out the window, I could barely see the parked NSA car through the stygian darkness. I wondered if Burrows and his fellow agents had slept any better. At least I had a comfortable bed, and contrary to what Woody had suggested and cajoled me about last night, when Barb and I finally hit the sheets any thoughts of lovemaking were traded for a warming cuddle and goodnight kiss.

The welcoming smell of coffee led me back to the kitchen. *I'll take some to the fellows in the car.*

Andy Hetzel also had a restless night, but an exciting one.

When he had driven to the local 7-Eleven to get some snacks and a few needed supplies his mother had overlooked, he had spotted Woody Floyd and Herschel Payne coming out of the convenience store. He guessed where they were headed and his guess was on target when the car drove down Kamilche Street and stopped in front of the Payne residence. Now it's the old "kill two birds with one stone" he had thought.

Andy had parked two blocks away on Kamilche and watched the house. Twice, a man he recognized as the driver of the car Hersch had been in came out of the house and walked to a car Andy hadn't noticed before, as it was parked on a side street. So there's at least two of them, probably three, he surmised. *I'll have to be careful.*

An hour later, Woody and the driver left the house and Andy followed them to their motel.

It was at that point he realized he now had two options: leave his little surprise at the Payne residence as had been his first plan, or catch most of them at the Plum Tree.

Time to wake up mother, he thought, as he temporarily put aside his planning and knocked on her door.

Agent Burrows had been sleeping soundly since completing his shift at the Payne's and returning to the Plum Tree. That was until the telephone rang. "Shit – it's barely daylight out!" he hollered in frustration. Burrows switched on the lamp and hoping it wasn't bad news, answered the persistent ring.

It was Frank Stiles from DC. They had an ID on Ki-woon's car. Then came the most startling information; Ki-woon was Andy's mother and there was a good chance he was now with her.

"All right," Burrows said, "Tell Harding I'm on it." He hung up. "Even if it is only five!"

Forty-One

Andy's bed was covered with the materials he needed. When he was a kid in Philadelphia, he and his buddy Ron Kerslace used to steal sulfur, charcoal, and potassium nitrate from a neighborhood Walgreen's drugstore and make gunpowder. Then when it got dark they poured a line of the gunpowder across a street in their neighborhood, waited until a car came, lit each side simultaneously and ran like hell. He figured making a bomb couldn't be that much more difficult, and besides he'd gotten some great recipes from a book at his local library.

Cutting off the heads of ten boxes of wooden matches was taking longer than he'd expected, and he thought he should have had his mother start on that project last night. The next step was to mix the chlorate, sugar and aluminum, then add the tetrachloride. The final two steps were to pack the pieces of pipe and add the fusing powder. He would have liked to use some kind of electronic detonator, but powder would have to do. He'd have to make sure the fuse was long and slow burning to give him time to get away. It was going to be a shame to use

Ki-woon's Chevy, but as he'd heard people say, "a bird in the hand is worth two …"

A knock at his door, followed by, "Andy, it's Mom."

She'd taken long enough, he thought as he unbolted and opened the door. "About time, here," he said, tossing her a box of Diamond stick matches.

"I still think this is a bad idea, we should get out of here this morning," Ki-woon said.

"You're up early," I said to Mark as he came into the kitchen.

"The 'early bird always catches the worm' you used to tell me, remember?"

I laughed. "Nope, can't say as I do, but that'll be important for you in the Navy."

"But that's how you caught Mom, you always said, being there before any of the other guys could steal her away."

"What's this – who stole who away," said Barb, walking into the room. "Hmm, coffee smells good."

Mark persisted. "You always told us that your buddy Ray didn't want to introduce Mom to you because you were 'too fast with the girls'."

"Fast, your father? Don't believe everything he tells you, maybe his car was fast, but him?" She smiled at me. "Besides, it was my beautiful songbird voice that hooked him."

The Cronus Cypher

"And it was my sharp-looking 1940 Chevy with the dual pipes and glass-packed mufflers that cinched the deal – not my good looks, I suppose?"

"Huh, I know what it really was that hooked you," Barb countered, "the classy brand new two-door '53 Chevy hardtop I was driving."

We hadn't heard Agent Burrows until he loudly cleared his throat. "I knocked, but no one answered, so …"

"Sorry, just some family reminiscing," I said. "What's up?"

"I'm going to get Woody in a minute, but thought I'd bring you up-to-date." He looked at Barb and Mark, as if to say shall I continue with them present.

"Go ahead, my family's part of this, and besides, I've brought them up to date – secrets or no secrets!"

"Okay. We've substantiated that the spy at the Seattle Korean legation, is named Ki-woon and, get this, for sure Ki-woon is Andy Hetzel's mother." He paused for effect. "Now, Ki-woon has eluded our guys in Seattle. Harding and Winslow think Andy may either be here already or on his way, and chances are, he'll hook up with Ki-woon and they'll flee the country together. We have a description and the license plate number of Ki-woon's car, and the local cops have been given the information. We also have men at the airport and at the border crossing in Blaine."

"So we're out of danger?" I asked.

"It would appear that way, but we'll stick around until we're absolutely certain."

205

"Why don't you stay and have a bite to eat," Barb said, "Hersch can give Woody a call and let him know you'll be awhile, besides it's still pretty early."

"Good idea," I offered. "Also, I need to stop in at the bank and touch base with my boss, make sure I still have a job. We can get Woody on the way back and he can probably use the extra sleep, anyway."

"Sounds like a plan," Burrows said, "and when you get done talking to Woody, I'll call the local sheriff – see if he has any news."

Andy watched as first Herschel Payne and then the person he figured was an NSA agent came out of the house, got into a car and drove down Kamilche Street. No sign of Woody, so Andy assumed they were on their way to get him at the Plum Tree Motel. He started the engine of the Catalina he'd stolen earlier off Whitney Pontiac's used car lot and cautiously followed.

He still hadn't completely made up his mind on whether to attack his enemies at the Payne residence or at the Plum Tree Motel. For now his mother's Chevy was parked behind the Town Center Motel and ready when he decided.

Forty-Two

Jacob Harding, Spence and Gerri stood in front of the TV set in Harding's office and watched Air Force One take off from Dulles.

"Well, they're on their way to Helsinki," Harding said. "Let's hope we get some results out of the conference." He switched off the TV and addressed Spence. "Is the support team ready to go?"

Spencer Winslow answered confidently. "Yes, we've narrowed it down to five men including Russ Collins, Chief Callgrove and Mick O'Brien. I'll act as supervisor. That should do it."

"Good. Any word from Seattle?"

"Yes. However, no sign of Hetzel or his mother Ki-woon. Our men are watching the house and the locals have been given Hetzel's description and the description of his mother's car."

"He's not stupid, and I doubt he'd be driving the car around if he is there, and I'd wager he's altered his appearance," said Harding. "But, sounds like we've done all we can for now."

The Navy man given the code name Zeus by the traitor Andy Hetzel and the man who years earlier had been blackmailed into being a co-conspirator, sat quietly in the Washington D.C. coffee shop weighing his options. His two friends were to join him in a few minutes.

He'd always thought the name Zeus an odd choice, being that the god Zeus in Greek mythology was the king of the gods and not subservient to anyone. Yet for years he'd been serving Andy, code name Cronus, whom Zeus had ultimately ruled over.

With Andy gone, the spy called Zeus no longer had the stomach for it. He made his decision. He would fulfill his obligation to his country and do what he could to make the Helsinki operation successful and then retire. No one would be the wiser and hopefully, he could someday forgive himself.

He looked up as his Navy buddies entered the shop.

"You ready to go to work?" Chief asked, sitting down across from him.

"I sure am, and glad all the intrigue and spy stuff is behind us."

"Me, too. Still, I wish Woody were here with us," Chief said.

"Yeah, I never could see him as that mole Cronus."

Forty-Three

His decision made, Andy had quickly driven the few blocks to the Town Center Motel and switched cars. He and Ki-Woon threw their things in the Pontiac Catalina and she followed him back to the Plum Tree.

When he got to the Plum Tree, it appeared his prey were there and there was still an open parking slot below the two rooms. If they had not been at the motel, he'd have gone with his second choice, the Payne house. He really didn't care as long as he got Herschel Payne, Woody Floyd, and as many of the NSA people as he could. His motives were now well beyond getting revenge for the killing of his grandparents, he wanted to punish those whom he fanaticized had ruined his life.

No one was in sight. *They must all be in the rooms.* He drove in the one-way lane, pulled into the parking spot and turned off the engine. *Still no one about.* Andy pulled out the Zippo lighter, reached behind the seat and lit the gunpowder fuse. He had estimated he would have two minutes and hopefully, that would be sufficient time for he and Ki-Woon to drive a safe distance and equally important that during the two minutes Hersch and others would still in be in harm's way. *Time to go.*

Andy got out and walked hurriedly to the Pontiac which Ki-Woon had pulled nearer at his signal. "Drive, get us out of here," he screamed at his mother.

Ki-Woon accelerated, turned left and …

"What's keeping them so long?" Woody asked me, as he rose and walked over to the clothes' rack near the door to get his coat. We were in Woody's motel room, which was next door to one of the rooms occupied by the NSA agents. I was sitting at the desk.

"Burrows must still be talking to DC." I answered. "It shouldn't be too long now."

The explosion was deafening. I was thrown off the chair and ended up on the floor between the two beds, which likely protected me from airborne sections of the outer wall and flying glass. At first I thought I'd been blinded, but realized I couldn't see because the air was thick with dust.

"Woody?" It sounded like my ears were full of water. For a second I flashed back to my first scuba diving try in Guam when I had come to the surface too quickly.

"Over here," I barely heard the voice I assumed was Woody's.

"Say again, I can't see."

Whether it was the breeze from outside due to the disappearance of the outer wall, I don't know, but the thick haze lifted long enough for me to get my bearings. I saw movement where once had been the door.

"Woody," I said again.

"Something is on top of me, I can't move."

"Hold on," I said, as I crawled around and over the debris. "Ouch!" I lifted my arm – blood ran from what looked to be a deep cut below my elbow. Under that, a piece of wood protruded.

I yanked out the splinter, ripped off a piece of nearby bed sheet, quickly fashioned a tourniquet, and continued crawling.

As I neared the area where I'd heard Woody's voice, I detected movement to my left and for the first time, realized the wall between the rooms was gone. I looked again to the left – no more movement and no sounds.

Woody was under the room's detached outside door and much like my being thrown between the beds; the metal door had acted as a shield. The door, however, was piled high with debris, including several pieces of the second floor railing and what could only be the hood of an automobile.

"I'm almost there," I shouted.

No response. Then I heard a hacking cough.

"Woody, I'll get this stuff off, just hang in there."

On the third try I realized the total weight was going to be too much for me. I had to shove the car hood off first.

I yelled for help. No one answered.

Ignoring the pain and throbbing in my arm, I pushed and finally the hood slid off the door. Woody's groan was almost drowned out by the sound of sirens.

As I used my good arm to remove a piece of the metal railing, a voice behind me said, "Here, let me help." It was agent Burrows, hardly recognizable behind his blood-streaked face.

Grays Harbor Community Hospital had never seen so many emergency patients at one time. Those with non-life-threatening injuries like me were sitting in the hallway while the others like Woody were being treated behind a row of curtained areas. In all, there were three dead, eleven with minor injuries and six in serious to critical condition. One of the dead was an NSA agent who had been in the room with Burrows.

The entire midsection of the Plum Tree had been blown asunder and the only reason there weren't more seriously injured was that the second story had not fallen in on the first. Two of the dead, who looked to be a man and a woman, had apparently been sitting in their Pontiac waiting for a delivery truck to finish and exit out the one-way drive. I'd overheard one of the doctors say that what remained of their bodies and that of the NSA man lay in the hospital's morgue.

Agent Burrows had just returned from talking on the phone to both the NSA Seattle agents and Harding in DC when I saw

Barb and the children coming down the hallway. I could see the concern on their faces.

"I'm okay, just a few cuts and bruises."

"Oh, you look fine," Barb said sarcastically, "if you had any more bandages you'd look like a mummy."

She looked at Burrows who was equally covered in dressings.

"How about Woody?" she asked, throwing her arms around me.

"A broken arm, several broken ribs and some nasty cuts, but he'll make it."

Melanie who at first had held back, probably at the sight of my bandaged body, rushed into my arms. Then the boys followed suit and we all hugged.

"Not too hard, guys, I hurt all over."

"Someone was watching over you, Dad," Bruce said, tears running down his cheeks.

"Yes. For a while I thought it was going to be like when I was about your age and got my arm stuck in a conveyor belt at Springfield Plywood. I yelled but no one came for at least five minutes."

Barb stepped back and looked at my left hand and smiled. "Wedding ring's still there."

I knew she was also remembering my accident at the plywood plant. The third finger on my right hand had been smashed so badly they had to cut off the plain gold ring she had given me.

"Yes it is, and this one, too," I said, holding out the right hand and showing her the ring she'd given me in 1953, the ring a jeweler had repaired so I could wear it again.

Burrows, who at this point hadn't said anything while my family and I consoled each other, tapped me lightly on the shoulder. "I'm going to check on Woody and the others."

I looked at Barb and she read my mind.

"You go ahead with Agent Burrows. We'll wait here for you."

Forty-Four

The "Helsinki Operations Team" had received several coded messages from Finland and Agent Spencer Winslow was pleased with how things had gone their first day. Now, well past midnight in Europe, he finished talking to Russ Collins and headed for the door. Everyone else had gone for the day. Russ alone would handle any communications until midnight DC time.

Spence was going to have a drink with Chief and Mick at the Blue Goose Lounge near their hotel and then meet Gerri for dinner at her place.

He spotted the two Navy men at the bar, each with a large mug of beer. "Hey, you guys didn't wait for me, I see."

"Nope, we figure you NSA types won't be covering our tabs much longer, so we need to stay ahead of the game," Mick said, downing his glass. "They've got Heineken on tap, too."

The bartender walked over. "Guess I'll join the crowd, I'll have a Heineken."

"So, you think it went well for the first day?" Chief asked Spence.

"Yes I do, very well."

"It's sure good we identified Andy as the mole before the conference," Chief continued. "Wonder where the hell he is now? Russ said Andy called himself 'Cronus', what a handle. Where'd he get a code name like that?"

"From Greek mythology, I imagine," Spence ventured. "In mythology Cronus was a really bad ass, so it's sort of fitting, I think, that he chose that name."

"Oh, here's your beer. First one's on us," Chief said.

Mick raised his glass. "Okay, here's to the team and Hersch and Woody."

The pager in Spence's pocket vibrated. He looked at the number. "I'd better take this, it's Harding."

When Winslow returned to the bar a few minutes later Chief and Mick could tell by his expression that something was wrong.

"You look like death warmed over," Mick said, it can't be that bad."

"It is – really bad." Spence took a large swig of his beer and told them what had happened in Montesano.

"My God," Chief said, "do they know what blew?"

"Not for sure, but Harding said there'd been some threats against the motel owner, something to do with one of the maintenance staff getting fired. I guess the guy was on parole and the manager found out and let him go. It looks like he might have set off a bomb in the parking lot next to the units. Harding said the latest should be on the news tonight." He checked his watch. "Let's see if we can get the bartender to turn on the television."

"You don't think Andy had anything to do with it do you?" Mick said.

Gerri turned away from watching TV and went to answer the doorbell ring. She rightly assumed it was Spence.

"I figured you'd be watching. What's the latest?" he said as he gave her a hug.

"What did you hear before you left Mick and Chief at the bar?"

"They were saying the local police think some irate ex-employee set off a car bomb and so far only three people are dead, but several are in serious condition."

"That's still about it. The reporter did say they think one of the dead may be the guy that set off the bomb. The local coroner is still trying to identify the remains."

"Anything said about our guys and NSA?"

"No," Gerri answered. "What's the latest from Larry Burrows, I assume you've talked to him again?"

"Still pretty upset about one of his men being killed, but Woody's going to be okay. He and Hersch are banged up, but not bad. They were plenty lucky."

"How about Hersch's family?"

"They're fine, at the hospital with Hersch, and the other one of Larry's team is still watching their house."

"No sign of Andy, I take it?"

"Nope." Spence sniffed. "That something burning?"

"Oh, damn! Dinner's probably going to be late, if at all," Gerri said, as she raced into the kitchen with Spence not far behind.

She pulled down the oven door. "Double damn!!" she said, "well it's late anyway, so how do salad and wine sound?"

"Sounds great to me, especially the wine. I had a beer with Chief and Mick, but I could definitely use a glass of red-eye, and salad will be great."

"**S**o how are Chief, Woody and Russ handling all this?" Gerri asked, when they'd cleared the dishes and returned to her living room.

"Okay, I think; didn't get a chance to call Russ at Fort Meade, but I assume he's heard about the explosion. Chief and Mick, they'll take it in stride – just happy their friends are okay."

"What about the Helsinki op, everything on schedule there?"

"Oh yeah, they were saying how glad they were that we'd exposed Andy as the mole Cronus."

Gerri set her wine down. "Who was saying that?"

"Ah … Mick and Chief – they'd been talking with Russ before I met them." Spence looked at Gerri questioningly. "Why, what's the big deal?"

"We never mentioned Andy's code name was Cronus to the op's team. Harding said we should keep them out of the loop. Only you and I, Woody, Hersch, Frank and Harding knew."

"That's right, so …"

"So one of them … no, that can't be. What <u>exactly</u> did Mick and Chief say?"

Spence contemplatively sipped his wine. "It was Chief, and he said that Russ told them Andy had called himself 'Cronus'."

"Russ said that?" Gerri said.

"Yeah, Russ. Shit, how did Russ know?"

"If Chief is telling the truth."

"Damn, and I was looking forward to some good …"

"So was I, but we'll just have to put that on hold lover boy."

Forty-Five

We left Woody at the hospital and headed home to Montesano, a very short drive compared to many we'd made as a family, the longest was in 1969. That year when I received orders for the base in Scotland, we drove across Morocco, by ferry to Spain, then to France, Switzerland, Germany, The Netherlands, Belgium, back to France, across to England by ferry and then to Scotland. Good old "Big John" had a few problems along the way but our trusty Chevy eventually got us there safe and sound.

"Remember our trip to Scotland?" I asked turning slightly to look at the kids in the back. Barb was driving.

"How could we forget," Mark said, "especially when you decided to replace us with the suitcases."

"What?" Then I knew what he was referring to. We were in Germany on the Autobahn when the car brakes failed and when I tried to stop by putting the car into Park, it came to a dead stop, throwing all our luggage from the rear compartment into the back seat.

The Cronus Cypher

Barb said, "You survived, and as I recall, you all thought it was great fun and yelled at your dad to 'Do it again Daddy'."

"We didn't."

"Yes you did. Now, here's our turn," said Barb taking the exit off Highway 8.

I glanced behind us. "Seems like déjà vu with a dark car following us – man, that seems like so long ago and yet it's been only a couple of weeks."

"So Mr. Burrows is still with us, huh?" Barb said, slowing for the stoplight.

"How long will the NSA guys be around?" Bruce asked.

"According to Agent Burrows, those 'guys' will stay at least two more days," I answered.

Harding got out of his car as Spence and Gerri pulled into the Fort Meade parking lot and stopped next to him.

"You'd better be right about this Winslow. It's been a long day and I needed some shut-eye bad!"

"Both Gerri and I think we are. Listen, Russ' shift ends pretty soon, so let me go over again what I told you on the phone and then you can decide."

"Fire away – and by the way, you'll both have to tell me sometime why you just happened to be together at Gerri's place so late in the day."

"What ...I ..."

"Don't say anything now – I mean, c'mon you two, it's pretty obvious there's something more than NSA business going on here, but forget that for now, tell me what you got."

Spence and Gerri went over every detail in the scenario which had convinced them Russ Collins was covertly tied to Andy, and thereby a part of a long established scheme to leak US secrets to the North Koreans.

"It explains how Andy got some of the information that he couldn't have had access to. Hersch had wondered about that. We always assumed Andy drugged people or got them drunk, and he might have, like Hersch in Scotland, but other times, he must have had help – it's the only thing that makes sense." Spence looked at his watch. "We're running out of time."

Harding nodded. "All right, I buy what you've said, but what the hell is Collins' motive, that's what really doesn't make sense."

"No idea," Gerri commented, "when we profiled him nothing popped out and when we quizzed Hersch in Montesano and Hersch interviewed him here, I don't recall anything that stood out other than the incident with the gay guy in Guam."

Another car pulled next to them and Frank Stiles got out.

Harding sighed deeply. "Guess we're ready. Frank, you armed, just in case?"

"Yes."

"Okay, I'll take the lead. Let's go."

The Cronus Cypher

Russ Collins had been expecting Mick O'Brien to relieve him for the next shift, and was surprised when Harding walked into the message control room accompanied by Winslow, Jennings and Frank Stiles.

"Hi guys, I thought Mick and maybe Chief were coming on duty, but this is impressive. Something must have happened to bring this entourage here at this late hour?"

Harding spoke first. "Something we needed to talk to you about, Russ."

"Yeah, sure, what's up?" Russ said, with a noticeable quiver in his voice.

"Russ, we could do with a few questions answered," Harding said. "Frank, if you will."

Stiles approached Russ. "Just stand still," he said and proceeded to pat down Russ.

Russ looked from Harding to Winslow, then at Jennings and when he saw the hard-faced expressions on their faces, his own turned a pasty white.

Stiles stepped back. "He's clean."

Shifting from one foot to the other and mumbling something unintelligible, Russ looked much like someone caught with their hand in the cookie jar.

"Sit down," Harding said forcibly to Russ. "Spence, go ahead."

Winslow sat in front of Russ, and leaning his face in so close that he could feel his quarry's breath, got right to the point. "How long have you been working with Cronus?"

"Cron …what?"

"You heard me, Cronus – like the Greek god – or better yet, how about Andy Hetzel!"

Russ looked at Winslow. "Oh my God …" He hung his head and all the life seemed to flow out of him – like a slowly deflating tire. "How'd you figure it out?" he finally said, and then like a light went on, "It was when I slipped up and mentioned the name Cronus to Chief and Mick."

"Why Russ, why in hell did you do this?" Spence said. "All these years – Russ you were trusted … your whole Navy career, all lies!"

Tears streamed down Russ' face, his chin rested on his chest, a shiver and then his whole body started to shake. "No, no, not all … oh damn … Andy Hetzel knew something about me, ah …caught me in … Guam … he would have told … oh my God, my wife … the …

Forty-Six

With every step taken my head reverberated, much like I remembered feeling after a night of one too many "screwdrivers", my drink of choice when I didn't know any better, and my arm felt like I'd gotten three extra batteries of vaccinations. Barb had redone some of the bandages so I didn't look like King Tut's twin, and scare my neighbors on my way to get the *Daily World*.

The headline and front page story chronicled yesterday's explosion at the Plum Tree, but in deference to Agent Larry Burrows and a call the managing editor got from Washington, D.C., no mention was made of the National Security Agency. The lead article did say that two of the injured were Montesano resident Herschel Payne who was there visiting his friend, and retired Senior Chief Petty Officer Woody Floyd, also injured and still in the hospital. The same article quoted Grays Harbor County Sheriff Franklin that preliminary investigations indicated a former employee of the motel set off the bomb and autopsies were being conducted on the three dead people.

I turned as Barb called from the front porch. "Hersch, c'mon, breakfast's ready."

Regardless of my injuries and concern for the others injured, I couldn't help feeling elated that the whole "Cronus" thing was likely behind me. The sun was shining, I could smell the freshly blossomed lilacs, I was home and my family was safe.

"Herschel, did you hear me, breakfast is getting cold and you've got a call from Agent Burrows."

My reverie disturbed, I stuck the morning paper under my arm and headed in.

Barb handed me the phone as I entered the kitchen, with a look that said, "See if I get up early and fix you your favorite breakfast again."

"Hello Larry, what's up?" I said, smiling at Barb in hopes that would make up for my tardiness.

I listened intently, shaking my head several times which I'm sure drove Barb crazy, especially when she saw my happy-go-lucky smirk disappear, replaced with one of sheer disbelief.

"Wow, that's really something, and right here in Montesano, we were sure lucky. And Woody's better? Great, tell him I'll be over later to see him. Oh, he can be released, super. Thank – oh, yeah, I'll have him call you. Same to you, Larry. Stop by on your way back, I'm sure Barb and the children will want to say goodbye and thank you. Too bad one of the guys had to die. Yeah, thanks again."

By the time I hung up, Barb was, as they say, "fit to be tied."

All she said was, "So!"

"First of all, as you heard, Woody is doing much better and we can pick him up any time after one today. But, here's the other news that's good, but weirdly good – the coroner identified the man in the car that blew – it was Andy Hetzel."

"Good God!"

"I know. Bowers figures he was trying to blow us all up at the motel and somehow didn't get far enough away when the explosion went. Maybe too short a fuse or perhaps he was blocked from exiting. I'm not really sure, but enough of the body was intact for them to finally conclude it was Andy."

"How's that?"

"The body had a German Eagle tattoo on one shoulder and a Scottish Lion on the other, but the clincher was the prints off of two of the fingers they found. Definitely Andy Hetzel." I shook my head. "I was with Andy when he got those tattoos in Scotland."

"The other person in the car?" Barb asked.

"Definitely a female – no positive ID yet. There's good chance it's the Seattle contact – his mother, Ki-Woon."

"So, it's over?"

"Yes, thankfully."

Our first breakfast together in some time as a family was interrupted ten minutes later.

"You get it this time, Hersch, it's probably for you anyway," Barb said as the phone rang for the third time.

"Hello – Spence, good to hear from you. Yes, did they call you about Andy?" I looked at Barb and nodded. "I'll say, we were lucky, and morbidly, Andy was not." I paused, shut up and listened when Spence said Andy was not why he was calling. Then with no fanfare, he told me about Russ Collins. Barb could likely tell by my expression the news was startling.

"Okay," I said a few minutes later. "I'll tell Woody, and Spence, thanks to you and Gerri for all you've done. "Seems like the end of a nightmare." Barb was waving at me. "Just a sec."

I listened to Barb's comment and passed it on. "Barb says to say hello to Gerri and she's welcome in her kitchen anytime. Oh, and she hopes you two will stop mooning at each other and do something about it."

I listened to Spence, then, "He says they already have." Barb gave me a thumbs up. "All right, bye for now, and thanks again."

Barb and the children who'd been taking everything in looked at me questioningly.

"Russ Collins was Andy's contact for years. That's how Andy got most of the top secret information. Unbelievable, but they confronted Russ with what evidence they had and he confessed."

"So all the bad people are caught"? Melanie asked.

"It looks like it," I said, "probably going to be real boring around here."

"Oh, I doubt that," Barb offered. "This is just another one of life's journeys and goodness knows we've been on a lot of those together – this one, especially for you, has been a journey of one and more.

Forty-Seven

Crossing the Baltic Sea by ferry in two hours, even in rough weather was for Hae-Won a welcome respite after the grueling ride to Quebec and then the fifteen hour Air Canada flight to Stockholm.

The two men were to meet her at the ferry terminal in Hanko from where they'd make the short drive to Helsinki. They would hold up a sign with her name, typical of something done when meeting tourists. She glanced at the passport – Yuriko Itami. Her father had always said she looked more Japanese than Korean.

She felt the boat slow and looked out the forward window. *Right on schedule. We will have just the right amount of time to drive there and set up. The Americans will think the Soviets did it, the English will think the Czechs, the Germans will blame the Poles ...*

Cronus will be proud of me!

The Cronus Cypher

230

Epilogue

The final act of the Conference on Security and Cooperation in Europe, known as the Helsinki Accords was the signing of the declaration in an attempt to improve relations between the Communist bloc and the West. The articles of confederation included: refraining from the threat of force, peaceful settlements of disputes and non-intervention in internal affairs.

U.S. President Gerald Ford reaffirmed that U.S. non-recognition of the Baltic States forced incorporation into the Soviet Union had not changed.

Unknown to the conference attendees was a thwarted attempt on President Ford's life, an assassination that if successful, would have thrown the conference into chaos as it would have surely been blamed on the Soviets. Although the captured culprits carried Albanian passports, under questioning one of the men revealed they were hired by agents of the North Korean government.

A female accomplice traveling with a Japanese passport eluded capture by NSA agents.

Acknowledgements and historical sources

Like my previous books, this novel could not have been written without the aid of many individuals. As stated in the introduction, *The Cronus Cypher* is extensively based on the memoirs of Melvin Williamson and during the creative stages of this novel Mel contributed additional background information as well as offering plot suggestions that have enhanced the tale. It was Mel's suggestion that we choose a family name, Payne, to be the last name of the lead character and his family.

My wife Jeanette contributed valuable insights as did my writer's group in Hoodsport, Washington, and as with my past three books, the final version could never have been successfully completed without my conscientious and thorough editor, Linda Steffen.

The Cuban missile crisis and ensuing blockade, the *Pueblo* incident in North Korea and the Conference on Security and Cooperation in Europe held in Helsinki, Finland are true historical events. References to an assassination attempt in

The Cronus Cypher

Helsinki are purely from my imagination as are the majority of the story lines involving the National Security Agency.

National Security Agency and the Explorer teams near the Demilitarized Zone did send warnings to the U.S. military about the major North Vietnam offensive that began on March 30, 1972, and U.S. air power became more effective in Vietnam after NSA succeeded in intercepting and jamming signals sent by the antenna of SAM missiles.

Thanks to Norm Beebe for providing a sample of the teletype tape used by machines like the 28-KSR.

There are no known facts to support the contention the North Koreans were given information on the course of the USS *Pueblo*. The crew was released on December 23, 1968.

Camp Weitek, Kami Seya, San Miguel, Kenitra and Ft. George Meade are real locations as are the other duty stations named in the story.

William Martin and Bernon Mitchell mentioned in Chapters eleven and twenty-one were code breakers for the National Security Agency and after four years as trusted employees, defected to the Soviet Union in June, 1960. There was wide speculation Martin and Mitchell were homosexuals but it was later revealed that they were not gay – just traitors who went to work for the Soviets. Mitchell was never in Rabat, Morocco and as far as is known, had nothing to do with the equipment on the U-2 airplane.

Mel Williamson did travel to the Shetlands twice, the second time participating in the parade group during Up-Helly-Aa celebration.

The Cronus Cypher

The towns of Satsop, Elma, Aberdeen and Montesano, Washington are real. However, if you have ever been to Montesano you know there isn't now nor has there ever been an Elephant Car Wash in the town. I couldn't resist putting the big, pink, iconic Seattle symbol into the story.

Elma and Montesano, Washington in Grays Harbor County have several popular eateries, including The Rusty Tractor and the Bee Hive restaurant.

I wasn't able to find a local winery that existed in Grays Harbor County in 1975. The reference to The Westport Winery is therefore thirty-three years premature.

The idea of the car bombing scene at the motel was inspired by an actual bombing that took place in Montesano in January of 1999. In the real incident a bomb packed with nails was detonated at the residence of *Daily World* writer and community corrections officer Tom Perrine. Mr. Perrine survived the blast.

The mythical deities Cronus and his wife Rhea were rulers of the world in the Golden Age. Cronus was the youngest of the Titans. Mythical Greek God names have arbitrarily been used as names for encryption systems in the U. S. Armed services. However, there is no knowledgeable history of Cronus being used in recent military crypto procedures.

The term "mole" first appeared in the *History of the Reign of King Henry VII* (1626) by Sir Francis Bacon. In modern times it is found in the novels of John le Carré. La Carré said in a BBC television interview in 1976 that it was a Russian KGB term.

Mel Williamson and his wife Bonnie live near Shelton, Washington. In his memoir dedication, Mel thanked Bonnie and his children Mark, Bruce and Melanie for their collaboration and support in his writing endeavor.

The Cronus Cypher is a collaborative effort of Mel Williamson, Frank Bishop and Hal Burton. It is primarily because of Frank Bishop's vision, inspiration, and continued support that this writing project was undertaken and successfully completed.

Hal Burton